Fruit Flies, Fish & Fortune Cookies

Avon Flare Books by
A.C. LeMieux

THE TV GUIDANCE COUNSELOR

ANNE LEMIEUX's first book, *The TV Guidance Counselor,* was an American Library Association Best Book for Young Adults. She was born and raised in Connecticut, where she lives in Black Rock with her husband and two children. This is her second book.

DIANE DE GROAT has illustrated over seventy books for children and won numerous awards. A graduate of the Pratt Institute, she lives with her husband and daughter in Chappaqua, New York.

Fruit Flies, Fish & Fortune Cookies

Anne LeMieux

Pictures by Diane de Groat

AN AVON CAMELOT BOOK

AVON BOOKS
A division of
The Hearst Corporation
1350 Avenue of the Americas
New York, New York 10019

Text copyright © 1994 by A.C. LeMieux
Illustrations copyright © by Diane de Groat
Published by arrangement with Tambourine Books, a division of William Morrow and Company, Inc.
Library of Congress Catalog Card Number: 93-29606
ISBN: 0-380-72291-7
RL: 4.9

First Avon Camelot Printing: August 1995

CAMELOT TRADEMARK REG. U.S. PAT. OFF. AND IN OTHER COUNTRIES, MARCA REGISTRADA, HECHO EN U.S.A.

Printed in the U.S.A.

OPM 10 9 8 7 6 5 4 3 2

To my daughter Sarah
with love

• • •

Special thanks to:
William Munsey,
Flight Experiments Mission Manager, NASA;
Mrs. Suellen Hansen,
who knows about fruit flies;
and Sarah LeMieux,
for her mercilessly meticulous editing!

TABLE OF CONTENTS

Best Pen Pals

1 · FORTUNE COOKIES

"REFLECT CAREFULLY TODAY, LEST YOUR DEEDS BRING BAD LUCK YOUR WAY." Mary Ellen Bobowick nibbled on the thumbnail of her right hand, frowning at the strip of white paper. "What kind of fortune is that?"

"Sounds more like a warning," Justine said. She carefully worked her chopsticks under a clump of steamed white rice and lifted it to her mouth.

"Well, it's stupid." Mary Ellen crumpled the fortune and tossed it toward the middle of the table.

Justine picked up the small paper wad, smoothed it out, and examined it closely.

"You better be careful, just in case, Mary Ellen. My aunt had a horoscope once that said something like 'Beware of a wild beast.' She just laughed at it because she lives in the city." Justine nodded mysteriously.

"So?"

"So the very next night she was going to the movies, and her taxi got rear-ended by a Jaguar. A *Jaguar*. Get it?"

"That's ridiculous. Could you pass the egg rolls?"

"It's not ridiculous." Justine pushed over the foil-lined bag with the last egg roll. "She had whiplash and had to wear this hideous foam-rubber turtleneck thing for three months."

"I don't mean your aunt getting hurt. I mean the horoscope. Predicting the future is totally unscientific." Mary Ellen scraped the shredded vegetables out of the egg roll with a chopstick. "Anyway, today's almost over. Whoever wrote this fortune wasn't thinking. It should say, 'Reflect carefully tomorrow.' No one eats fortune cookies for breakfast."

"Don't be so picky. 'Tomorrow' doesn't sound

as good. Besides, it doesn't rhyme with 'way.' What are you doing?"

Mary Ellen was holding up the hollow egg roll wrapper and carefully squeezing the last of three packets of duck sauce into it.

"Chinese jelly doughnut." She took a big bite and a glob of the sweet orange sauce rolled down her chin. She wiped it away with the back of her hand. "Mmm. Good. Want some?"

Justine made a face. "Ugh. Would you mind not being completely disgusting?" She pushed a stack of napkins over and cracked open her own cookie. "Hey, listen to mine: A STITCH IN TIME SAVES THREAD. Someone must have been getting tired at the fortune cookie factory. I could write a better fortune than that. Is there any more sesame chicken?"

Mary Ellen popped the other half of the egg roll in her mouth, then slid the cardboard carton across the table. As Justine turned it upside down on her plate, Mary Ellen giggled.

"What's so funny?" Justine asked.

"I was just thinking, you could do that for your Career Day report. 'When I grow up, I want to write fortunes in a cookie factory.' I wonder if they pay by the hour or the fortune."

"Go ahead and laugh. I bet I'd be good at it. I'd only write great ones."

"Like, 'A tall dark handsome stranger will come into your life?" Mary Ellen teased.

Justine nodded. "Speaking of tall dark handsome strangers, what do you think of that new kid, Ben?"

Mary Ellen crossed her fingers mentally. "I didn't really notice him."

"How could you not notice? He's gorgeous. What a tan. A California tan."

"He should use sunscreen. Dark tans aren't healthy."

"They sure look good, though!"

Leaning over her plate, Mary Ellen dissected the shredded egg roll debris with her chopsticks. "Anyway, it's not like he'd ever notice me. Boys don't go for the string-bean type."

"You're not a string bean," Justine said loyally. "You're more of a —" She bit her lip.

"Toothpick? That's what Jason wrote on the board yesterday morning. 'Toothpick Bobowick.' He's torturing me already, and it's only the first week of school."

"Jason's a jerk—and he should talk, anyway, with his teeth. He looks like a horse."

"Yeah, but he has braces. He won't always have horse teeth. I can't do anything about being so skinny."

"Well, being thin is better than being like me. Look at these thunder thighs." Justine pinched her leg through her blue jeans.

"That's because you're sitting down. Everyone has thunder thighs sitting down, because legs spread out," Mary Ellen said. She looked at her own lap. "Everyone except me. And at least you have something on the top to balance out the bottom."

"Some people develop slower than others."

"Easy for you to say. You're not stuck wearing one of those elastic bras they make because someone's too old for an undershirt, but too flat for a real bra." Mary Ellen smoothed her shirt down. "Look."

"Look at what?"

"Exactly. There's nothing to look at. I'm an ironing board. I'm a pancake. I'm practically concave. I hate myself."

"Mary Ellen, you have to stop that. You can't hate yourself. My sister has this book called *You're the Only Self You've Got.* Maybe you should read it."

"No thanks. Anyway, I didn't mean I hate

myself. I just hate the way I look."

"Well, if you're not happy with how you look, maybe you could do something. Change something."

"Like what? What can I do to make myself look different? I can't exactly erase my freckles." Mary Ellen gnawed on her pinkie nail.

"Well for one thing, you could stop biting your nails. Especially when you're eating. That's like cannibalism or something."

"It's just extra protein. That's what fingernails are made of. And you used to chew your hair." But she snatched her hand away from her mouth.

"Well, I don't anymore." Justine smoothed down her blond hair with one hand. "And you could cover your freckles with some foundation if you don't like them."

"It's no use. I'd still be stuck with the rest of me." Mary Ellen picked up the carton of chicken fried rice, then put it down. "I'm full. Want the rest?"

"I'm never full. I guarantee I'll be starving in an hour. But I absolutely refuse to have another bite." Justine looked down at her empty plate, and groaned. "Did I really eat all that?" She shook her head, stood, and began to clear the table.

"We don't have to do that now. My mother said

they won't be home from your parents' party till midnight." Through the open window, Mary Ellen could hear the party noise, music, and the buzz of a bunch of conversations going on at once. All the grown-ups in the neighborhood were invited.

"If we do it now, we won't have to do it later," Justine said. "Besides, I need to work off some of these calories. Did you know Chinese food has an incredible amount of fat in it? Maybe you could try a Chinese-food diet."

"It wouldn't work. It's my metabolism. I have a fast metabolism. I probably burn more calories chewing than there are in what I eat." Mary Ellen sighed and piled the leftovers on her plate. As she stood up, the toe of her sneaker caught on her chair leg.

"Aaagh!" she yelped, stumbling, fumbling the plate and just barely catching it before it tipped and spilled. "Whew! That was a close one."

Justine giggled.

"It's not funny," Mary Ellen said.

"I wasn't laughing at you," Justine apologized. "I was thinking of something my mother told me. When she was in seventh grade, she took ballroom dancing lessons. You know, that old people stuff? The teacher used to tell the girls that whenever they entered a room, they should hold their heads up, walk like this, and say over and over, 'I'm beautiful, I'm lovely—I like everyone and everyone likes me.'" Demonstrating, Justine held out her arms and glided across the kitchen.

Mary Ellen laughed. She could picture Mrs. Kelly doing that, even now. Then she shook her head. "It wouldn't work for me. If I held my head up, I'd probably trip and fall flat on my face. When I go into a room, I automatically think, 'I'm horrible, I'm skinny—it doesn't matter who I like because I'll never get a boyfriend.'"

"What about Kevin Middendorf? He had a crush on you all last year."

"Kevin Middendorf eats peanut-butter-and-pickle sandwiches for lunch every day. Can you imagine kissing him?"

"*Eeee-ew!*" Both girls squealed, then burst out laughing.

"See? There are worse things than no boyfriend at all," Justine said. "Besides, Olivia says you should never define yourself by your relationship with a man."

"Easy for her to say," Mary Ellen commented. Justine's sister had more guys hanging around her than ants at a picnic.

Justine emptied the last bit of gummy rice into the almost full compost container in the sink. "Are you going to put this out now?" she asked Mary Ellen.

Mary Ellen looked out the kitchen window. Next to the Bobowicks' garage was the compost heap, a mound of decaying garbage that her mother used as fertilizer for their vegetable garden. By the yellow glow of the garage spotlight, she could see a bulky brown waddling shadow.

"Uh-uh." She shook her head. "Look."

Justine leaned over to see. "Raccoon? Wow! It's practically as big as a Saint Bernard."

"That's from pigging out on our garbage every night. They think it's their own private buffet. I'll let my dad put this out when he gets home."

"Here, I'll wipe the table while you load the dishwasher." She reached around Mary Ellen for the sponge.

Mary Ellen stacked the rinsed dishes in the dishwasher, then turned around just in time to see Justine about to toss the chopsticks in the trash.

"Wait! Don't throw those away!"

"Mary Ellen, they're disposable. They give you new ones every time."

Mary Ellen snatched them from her and

scrubbed them under the running water.

"You're a pack rat, you know that?" Justine said.

"I am not. I'm a recycler. You never know what'll come in handy."

"How could two pairs of used chopsticks possibly come in handy?"

Mary Ellen twiddled the chopsticks with her fingers while she thought.

"Hair things!" she said after a minute. "See?" She twisted her brown hair into a bun and stuck the sticks through the middle.

Justine snorted. "Very chic, Mary Ellen. But you know—" She stopped and tilted her head. "Your hair looks pretty, up like that, pulled back from your face. Hey, why don't we give you a makeover?"

Mary Ellen eyed her doubtfully. "Isn't there some saying that you can't make a pocketbook out of pig's feet or something?"

"What does that have to do with it? We're not going to make a pocketbook. We're going to make a new you. Come on." Justine tugged on her sleeve.

"My mother doesn't have as much makeup as yours. Like purple mascara, and gold eyeshadow and—"

"You don't need all that," Justine said impatiently. "We'll start with the basics. Hey, maybe we should give you a facial first. Olivia uses this all-natural recipe with honey, oatmeal, and raw egg whites."

"Your sister actually puts that on her face? Talk about disgusting. I may be messy, but you won't catch me with raw egg on my face."

"It's not the whole egg, it's just the whites," Justine said. "And you whip them up first, like meringue."

"We just cleaned the kitchen." Mary Ellen knew that would decide Justine.

"Okay. Just a makeover then. Let's go."

Mary Ellen followed Justine upstairs. She grabbed her mother's small cosmetic case and her antique silver brush-and-mirror set. At the door to her own bedroom, she caught Justine making a face.

"Don't say it," she said. "I know. But at least I cleared off the bed you're sleeping in."

"If I can make it across the room without breaking my neck! How do you ever find anything in here?"

"I have my own system. Anyway, the light's better in the bathroom. Let's go in there." Mary Ellen headed down the hall.

In the bathroom, she set the mirror and brush down on the vanity counter, next to the sink.

"Those are really pretty," Justine said.

"They were my mother's great-grandmother's." Mary Ellen traced the ornate design on the back of the brush with her finger, while Justine unpacked the small collection of cosmetics and carefully laid everything out next to the mirror.

"How can someone be so neat automatically?" Mary Ellen asked in amazement.

Justine shrugged. "I don't know. My dad says 'Organization is power.' But I don't think about it. I can't help it any more than you can help being messy."

"My mother says 'Clutter is the sign of a creative mind,'" Mary Ellen told her.

"Fine! So I'm dull but neat. Now sit."

Mary Ellen sat on the toilet cover while Justine studied her seriously. "We'll start with some light foundation to cover your freckles." Justine opened the beige bottle. "Tilt your head up," she ordered. "And don't squint like that."

"But the light's in my eyes." Mary Ellen turned sideways. "There, that's better."

Justine began to dab the liquid makeup on her cheeks. "We should give you a manicure too. Does your mom have any nail polish?"

"Only clear, I think."

"Well, that'll be okay. Bright red might look kind of funny with your nails all bitten. I thought you made a New Year's resolution to stop that," Justine said.

"I thought you made one not to be so critical."

"Okay, okay. It's for your own good, though. Anyway, we can soak your nails while I work on your face."

Mary Ellen wrinkled her nose. "You make it sound like some kind of construction project."

"Stop that." Justine tapped Mary Ellen's nose with her finger. "It is. We're building the new you. Do you have any of that dish-washing liquid, the kind the lady on the commercial uses?"

"Uh-uh. Only environmentally friendly stuff. Should I go get it?"

Justine pursed her lips and looked around the bathroom, then leaned over the tub and grabbed a bottle of chamomile baby shampoo. "No. This should be mild enough."

Mary Ellen put down the drain stopper, poured half the bottle into the sink, then plunged her hands into the thick yellow liquid. "How long do they have to soak?"

"A few minutes, I guess. Don't talk. Hold still, I want to do your eyes now. Look down."

Mary Ellen looked at her sneakers obediently and tried not to blink. The eye-shadow brush tickled her eyelids, which for some reason made her feel like sneezing.

"It's going to come out uneven," Justine warned.

Mary Ellen held her breath to keep from moving and tried not to blink. Justine stepped back and surveyed the results.

"How do models ever do this all day long? It's torture," Mary Ellen said.

"It just takes practice. Okay," Justine said. "Now mascara. You better put that on yourself; I don't want to poke your eye out." She held out the mascara wand and the hand mirror.

Without thinking, Mary Ellen reached for them with her shampoo-coated hands. A second later there was a crash, and the mirror was face down on the tile floor. Shards and slivers of silvered glass were everywhere.

Both girls gasped. Mary Ellen's stomach felt as if it had dropped through the toilet seat.

"Uh-oh," Justine said nervously. "Will your mother be really mad?"

Mary Ellen swallowed and looked at the mess.

"Upset is what she'll be, I think."

Suddenly Justine clutched Mary Ellen's arm. "Do you know what this means?"

"What?"

"Seven years of bad luck!"

"Are you trying to make me feel even worse?" She shook Justine's hand off.

"But the fortune—"

"Just shut up, will you? That's an idiotic superstition!" The sick feeling in Mary Ellen's stomach got worse, as if the chicken she'd eaten had come back to life and was pecking at the fried rice.

"Well, where do you think superstitions come from, anyway?" Justine put her hands on her hips, talking in the superior know-it-all way that Mary Ellen hated.

"They come from the Dark Ages, when everyone thought the world was flat, and no one knew squat about science!" Mary Ellen's voice was getting louder.

"You don't have to yell at me, Mary Ellen. Olivia says a lot of folk wisdom got lost when everything went modern. She has this astrology book—"

"I don't want to hear about your weird sister's weird books."

"My sister is not weird!" Now Justine was shouting too.

"Anyone who eats tofu voluntarily is definitely weird." Mary Ellen folded her arms across her chest and glared.

"Oh yeah? Tell that to bazillions of Japanese people who eat it every day!" Justine glared back. "And look who's talking. Your brother eats bugs!"

"He only ate half a caterpillar once! When he was two years old!"

Then both girls looked down at the broken mirror at the same time. Mary Ellen's shoulders sagged.

"Oh," she whispered.

Justine bit her lip. "I'll go get the broom."

2 · BAD LUCK

Without getting out of bed, Mary Ellen stretched over and switched on her aquarium light. As the fluorescent light flickered, then winked on, her four tiny damselfish darted out from the rock caves where they slept. Or spent the night, anyway. Mary Ellen didn't know if fish actually slept. She'd never seen one with its eyes closed.

Two of hers were black-and-white striped, one was bright blue, and the other was blue with a gold tail. Flipping the tank lid up, she sprinkled a pinch of food flakes in. The flakes sifted down through the water like khaki-colored snow. Mary

Ellen rolled over on her stomach and watched her fish chase their breakfast.

Reaching over the side of the bed, she groped between the mattress and box spring—where she kept important things so they wouldn't get lost in her room—and pulled out a lab notebook from the Dickerson University bookstore. It was navy-blue, with silver letters embossed on the cover, the kind all her mother's students used in the biology classes she taught. Opening to a clean page, Mary Ellen started her daily entry.

Saturday, September 9
1. Observations
   1. I think fish might be smarter than people realize. When I turn the light on, they get all excited and swim up to the top of the tank.
2. Questions
   1. Do fish recognize a person, like their owner?
   2. Can you train fish?

That might make an interesting experiment. She could make a hoop by cutting out a plastic coffee-can top, and hold some food on the other side with tweezers. Maybe they'd learn to swim through it.

She made a note:

> 3. Experiment
>   1. Set up behavioral experiment with hoop swimming.

Mary Ellen surveyed the page with satisfaction. Her room might be messy, but her lab notebook was perfect. Even her numbers were perfect. She made them look like they were typed. Turning back to the tank for further observation, Mary Ellen watched her fish lunge at the flakes. The flakes made her think of cereal. Her stomach growled. Breakfast time. She kicked off the covers, then slipped the notebook back under the mattress. Rolling out of bed, she picked a path across the room, tiptoeing around all the stuff on the floor.

"Are you awake?" She whispered to Justine.

"Mmmmph," Justine mumbled, without opening her eyes.

Mary Ellen shook Justine's shoulder. "Don't you want breakfast?"

"No! I want to sleep. Saturday's the only day I can sleep till a decent hour." Justine tugged the covers over her head.

Mary Ellen's stomach growled again. Her

appetite was definitely awake. Justine could waste the whole day if she wanted to; Mary Ellen wanted food.

As she was halfway down the stairs, she heard her mother's voice float up from the kitchen. "But it's so sudden. I don't see how Corinne can possibly do it so quickly."

Mary Ellen stopped in mid-step. What did Justine's mother have to do quickly?

"You know what Walter always says—all it takes is organization," her father said.

"I wonder how Justine will feel, being pulled out of school three weeks into the year," her mother went on. "Eleven is a hard age to be uprooted like that."

"I think moving to Paris will make up for—" Mary Ellen's father was saying, but she didn't hear the rest. Her knees sagged and she clutched the banister. Moving to Paris?!

She crept back up to her room and curled up in her quilt. She stared across at Justine, who was still asleep. How could something so terrible happen?

Last night's accident popped into her head, along with the words of her fortune: REFLECT CAREFULLY TODAY, LEST YOUR DEEDS BRING BAD LUCK YOUR WAY. Mirrors reflected. She hadn't reflected carefully and the mirror broke. That could be the deed. And now, here was the worst luck she'd ever had, her best friend moving to Paris. And Justine hadn't even told her. Mary Ellen buried her face in the pillow.

A few minutes later she heard her mother's footsteps and cheerful voice.

"Time to rise and shine, girls."

Mary Ellen turned her head and opened one eye. Sunlight poured in as her mother twitched open the blinds. She pulled the quilt over her head, but could hear Justine yawning.

"Morning, Dr. Bobowick. How was the party? I helped make the hors d'oeuvres."

"It was a wonderful party, and the hors d'oeuvres were spectacular. Hop up, Justine. Your parents want you home right away. They have some exciting news."

"What exciting news?"

Mary Ellen heard the swish of sheets and blankets and the thump of feet on the floor as Justine got up.

"It's not my news to tell, honey," said Dr. Bobowick.

The side of Mary Ellen's bed sagged as her mother sat down on the edge.

"Daddy bought bagels from the bakery. They're on the table, so get 'em while they're fresh." Her mother patted her on the shoulder through the quilt, then rose. Mary Ellen listened to her leave.

"What could be so exciting?" Justine sounded mystified. "Nothing exciting ever happens around here."

Mary Ellen didn't say anything until they were dressed and downstairs in the kitchen. She went straight to the back door, yanked it open, and held it. "You better go find out what that exciting news is."

Justine stared. "Fine! See you later. Grouch!"

Mary Ellen slammed the door behind Justine. She went over to the sink and looked out the window in time to see Justine duck through the hole in the hedge between the two houses. Outside, Mr. Bobowick was crisscrossing the lawn with the mower, his lips pursed in his regular yard work whistle. How could he be so cheerful on such a horrible morning? She turned away, walked listlessly to the table, picked up a butter knife, and stabbed a bagel.

"You weren't being very nice to Justine just now. Did you girls have a fight?" Dr. Bobowick was standing in the doorway of her study, the small room off the kitchen that might have been a maid's room if they'd had a maid. She was frowning.

Mary Ellen looked up at her mother and tears brimmed in her eyes. "Are the Kellys really moving to Paris?"

"Ahhhh. I see." Her mother's frown softened into a sympathetic look, and she came over and sat beside Mary Ellen.

"Mr. Kelly got a consulting job, just for one year. They're moving, but they're not selling the house, only renting it. And they'll be back next August, in time for you and Justine to start junior high together."

"But a year? That's—that's almost ten percent of my whole life!"

"So far," Dr. Bobowick said, nodding. "But just think, if you live to be a hundred, it will only be one percent."

The tears spilled over and trickled down Mary Ellen's cheeks. Her mother put an arm around her shoulders and gave her a squeeze.

"A year's not forever, honey."

"No, but it feels like it, when it's stretching out in front of you." Mary Ellen sniffed and wiped her eyes on her sleeve.

A year was a long time. Seven years was even longer, especially if it was going to be filled with luck like this. Was it possible to be the victim of a superstitious curse, even if you didn't believe in that stuff? Mary Ellen wondered if her mother had found the mirror yet, face down on her dresser, under a scarf, where she'd put it last night. She might as well get it out of the way now. No matter how upset her mother got, the day couldn't get any worse.

"I broke your mirror last night," she confessed, poking her index finger into a blob of butter on her plate and swirling it around. "Your good one. Justine was making me over, and I dropped it. I'm sorry."

She didn't look up until her mother reached over and pulled her finger out of the butter.

"I hope neither of you cut yourself."

Mary Ellen shook her head. "Aren't you mad?"

Her mother smiled. "Have you ever noticed the dent near the bouquet on the top? I was doing an experiment when I was about nine, trying to burn a hole in a leaf by reflecting sunlight. I dropped the mirror on the sidewalk. So the glass wasn't original. It can be replaced."

"Oh." Well, that was a relief, anyway. Mary

Ellen poured a glass of orange juice from the pitcher on the table and took a sip.

"Why would you want to make yourself over?" Dr. Bobowick asked. "What's wrong with the way you are? I think you're practically perfect."

Mary Ellen took another sip and managed a small smile. "Like Mary Poppins? Not quite. And anyway, you have to say that. You're my mother."

Dr. Bobowick stood, leaned over, and dropped a quick kiss on the top of Mary Ellen's head.

"I just analyze the data as I see it, sweetie. And speaking of data, if I don't get my lab reports graded, I'm going to have to flunk myself. Can you get the phone if it rings? I'm not available unless it's an emergency."

Mary Ellen nodded, then stuck a finger through her bagel half and started nibbling it all around the edge, wondering what it would be like in school without Justine. They'd been best friends since they were three, started kindergarten together, and always been in the same class. Not to mention being next-door neighbors for eight years.

She ate the bagel down to a ring, then stuck her tongue through the ring and mashed it around in her mouth until the last bit melted away. She thought about going over to the Kellys', but she didn't know what to say to Justine. Maybe she didn't even want to go to Paris. Maybe they were having a huge fight about it right now. Better wait.

Mary Ellen wandered over to her mother's study. After a minute, Dr. Bobowick looked up.

"What is it, honey?"

"Mom, why don't I just quit sixth grade and come to Dickerson with you? I mean, why do I have to spend years stuffing my brain with useless information when I already know I want to be a biologist? And you're a teacher, so it would count legally as going to school, wouldn't it?"

Her mother tilted her head and smiled.

"Don't you think you'd miss out on a lot if you jumped from sixth grade right to college?"

"Like what? Years of torture?"

"Like slumber parties with your friends, and graduations and the feeling of accomplishment that goes with them. All kinds of things. Your junior prom—"

"The statistical odds of me being invited to the junior prom are probably negative numbers."

Dr. Bobowick shook her head emphatically. "False conclusion from a faulty hypothesis." She leaned back in her chair. "Mary Ellen, I know it's going to be a little rough getting used to not having Justine at your side. But maybe it'll be a good chance for you to broaden your scope of friendships."

"I don't want to broaden my scope of friendships. Best friends aren't just interchangeable."

"I know that." Her mother smiled. "But if you let this color your whole outlook, you'll talk yourself into a miserable year. If I were you, I'd think about putting aside my own feelings and trying to be happy for Justine."

"How can I be, when she's deserting me?"

"It's not as if she has a choice. And it's a wonderful opportunity for her. So try not to make her feel too bad. Now, I have to get these reports done. I'm going to run over to campus after lunch. Would you like to come with me?"

"I guess so." Actually, the thought of going to the bio lab at Dickerson cheered her up a little. All that equipment, the specimens and books, beakers and test tubes, scales and microscopes.

"Can I look at some slides?"

"Yes, you may look at some slides."

Mary Ellen turned to leave, then turned back one more time.

"Mom?"

Now her mother looked slightly impatient. "Yes, honey?"

"We have to do a report for Career Day in school next week. Oral reports, and we have to bring something that has to do with our chosen career. What should I bring?"

"How about one of my lab coats? I can give you an old badge and you can glue one of your school pictures to it," Dr. Bobowick suggested.

"But a lab coat could look like a doctor or a dentist." Mary Ellen frowned.

"Well, I'm sure you'll think of something. I'll help you later. Now, shoo. Please." Dr. Bobowick turned back to her papers and Mary Ellen knew enough not to disturb her further at that point.

She went back to the table and sat there glumly. The screen door slammed again. Was Justine back? Mary Ellen turned in her chair. No—it was Nicky; her little brother had spent last night at Gram's house.

"We're ho-ome."

"So I hear," said Dr. Bobowick, coming into the kitchen.

Nicky bounded across the room and tackled their mother with a hug.

"Look-it, Mommy, look-it, Melon!" He

dropped Dizzy, his stuffed lizard, on the floor, then spun on one foot and kicked the air. "*Kee-ai!* YAH!"

Mary Ellen's grandmother came in a moment later with Nicky's overnight bag. Dr. Bobowick looked at her. "*Kee-ai?* Could you translate that for me, Mother?"

"It's karate talk for 'watch out,'" Nicky explained. "Gram's teaching me." He grabbed a bagel from the plate still on the table and sank his teeth into it.

"Karate talk?" Dr. Bobowick repeated, raising her eyebrows.

"Oh, didn't I mention the new class I'm taking at the Y?" Gram asked innocently. But her round cheeks were pink and Mary Ellen could see laughing glints in her eyes. "I thought I told you."

"No," Dr. Bobowick said. She put her hand to her chin and shook her head. "No. I'm quite sure I would have remembered if you had told me you were taking a karate class." Mary Ellen could tell she was upset.

Her grandmother glared. "Now before you say anything, Laura, let me tell you one thing. I refuse to resign myself to a life of boring bridge games or—or—bingo! I'm not going to let old age sneak up on me, and if it tries, I'm going to be ready to give it a good fight. *Kee-ai!* So there!"

Mary Ellen stifled a giggle. Dr. Bobowick stared for a long moment, then threw her hands up.

"It's your life," she said. "And your limbs, I might add."

"Right," Gram said. "It is and they are."

Mary Ellen's mother shook her head, but she finally smiled. "Well, I don't know about the wisdom of teaching a four-year-old the martial arts, but thanks for taking him last night. Did he behave?"

"Sure I did," Nicky piped up. "Gram said if I was good, she'd teach me karate. *Kee-ai!* YAH!"

"Not in the house, Nicholas Bobowick," Gram said. "That was our deal. Next time I'll teach you how to combine a back kick with your roundhouse. Well, I've got to run. *Kee-ai!*" Gram chopped the air, then waved, and left.

"Can I watch cartoons?"

Dr. Bobowick closed her eyes and nodded. "For a little while."

"Yay! *Kee*-yay!" Nicky kicked and whirled toward the den.

Mary Ellen heard Gram rev her engine, then

peel out of the driveway with a slight screech. Dr. Bobowick opened her eyes and put one hand to her forehead. Mary Ellen grinned at her mother.

The back door slammed for the third time that morning, as Justine burst in. "What do you want first, the good news or the bad news?" she asked breathlessly.

From behind Justine, Mary Ellen's mother gave her an encouraging nod, and pulled her mouth into a smile with two fingers.

Mary Ellen sighed, then forced a smile of her own. "The good news."

3 · FRIENDS & FIGHTS

"You are so lucky, Justine. I can't believe you get to ditch this dump and spend the whole year in Paris," Amy Colter said.

"In Paa-ris," Mary Ellen echoed in a singsong voice, wrinkling her nose.

"What?" Justine, sitting between them, swung around and looked at Mary Ellen.

"Nothing," Mary Ellen muttered.

"Grow up, Mary Ellen," Amy said. She shook her head, then pulled a compact out of her purse, flipped it open, and checked herself out in the tiny mirror. And smiled at herself. She actually smiled at herself. Mary Ellen rolled her eyes.

"My father says we're going to live on the Left Bank. It's kind of like the Village in New York City," Justine went on.

"That is *so* cool. Hey, maybe I could come visit you. Like on vacation or something."

"That would be fantastic," Justine said. "Do you think your parents would let you?"

"I'll ask. Oooh, shopping in Paris," Amy squealed. "That would be even better than the mall!"

Mary Ellen couldn't believe it. Last year Amy had given a slumber party and invited half the class. The cool half. Neither she nor Justine had been included then. Talk about a phony!

She clamped her teeth into her slice of soggy school pizza and tore off a piece. Ever since Justine had found out the so-called exciting news, it was Paris this and Paris that and Paris, Paris, Paris.

"Could we talk about something else? Or someplace else? Like Outer Mongolia or Timbuktu?" Mary Ellen made her voice sound as bored as possible.

"You're just jealous, Mary Ellen," said Debra Hirsch. Mary Ellen saw her glance across the table at Amy, as if she wanted to see if she scored a point or something. Amy nodded at her.

Mary Ellen couldn't refrain from snorting. What were those animals that followed each other off a cliff every year? Lemmings. Debra was a lemming.

"I'm not jealous. Who wants to go to stupid old Paris, with all those French people jabbering zis and zat and ooh-la-la? I don't."

"Ignore her, Justine," Amy said.

Justine sniffed and turned back toward Amy. "My mother said I could get a perm if I want. I think I'll wait till we get there and have it done by a Parisian hairdresser."

"You'll probably come out looking like a French poodle!" Mary Ellen gave Justine a fake smile. There, score one for her.

"Don't be such a snot, Mary Ellen," Debra said.

"If you don't want to listen, why don't you leave?" Amy looked down her stupid powdered nose at Mary Ellen.

"I think I will." Acting as casual as she could, Mary Ellen stood with her tray and nudged her chair into the table with her foot. As she tried to squeeze through the narrow passage between their table and the next, her tray slipped. She clutched it so it wouldn't fall, and what was left of her pizza flopped against the front of her pink blouse, leaving a greasy orange smear.

"Nice one, Toothpick!" Jason Hodges snickered. He elbowed the new kid, Ben, who grinned.

"Why don't you just shut up, Tinsel Teeth?" Mary Ellen plowed into his chair, trying to get by.

Jason jerked his elbow up, hitting her tray, and the pizza scrap flipped off onto the floor.

"Oh, ex-*cuuuse* me!" Now everyone at both tables was laughing.

"So, Mary Ellen, are you going to do your Career Day report on being a waitress? Good luck to your customers," Amy smirked.

Furious, Mary Ellen shoved Jason's chair in, stepped over the glop, and started to walk away.

"Aren't you even going to clean that up?" Debra called after her. "Someone could slip and break their neck, you know."

"Forget it," Mary Ellen heard Justine say loudly. "You should see her room—a total pigsty."

Mary Ellen froze at the words. What a traitor! Whirling around, she opened her mouth, but she couldn't think of a comeback.

"Whoa, watch out, Justine! She looks mad now," Jason warned. He turned to Mary Ellen. "Your face is so red you look like a big strawberry," he said, then elbowed Ben again. "Doesn't she?"

"Especially with those dots." Ben was nodding and grinning.

Dots? Living with freckles was bad enough, but to have them labeled *dots* by some new kid with a California tan was too much. She glared at Ben, who dropped his eyes, almost as if he felt a little ashamed. But he was still smiling, and Jason and the other boys were laughing so hard they were falling off their seats.

Fuming, Mary Ellen fled the cafeteria for the girls' room. She hid in a stall, waiting for the bell to ring and everyone to leave.

The blouse stain couldn't have been in a more embarrassing place. Scrubbing with water and paper towels didn't help at all, it only added a big wet spot that let the outline of her stupid baby underwear show through.

By the time she got back to class, clutching a notebook to her chest to try to hide the damage, Ms. Purcelli-Smith was passing out a pop math quiz.

"You're late, Mary Ellen." Her teacher, the shortest in the school, had to look up at Mary Ellen this year.

"Sorry," Mary Ellen mumbled, sliding into her

seat with her shoulders hunched. At least Ms. P. S., as everyone called her, wasn't the yelling type, which Mary Ellen knew from last year. She'd been their fifth-grade teacher, but she got promoted along with her class when Mr. Thompson, the sixth-grade teacher, decided to take a year off to bike around the whole United States.

In a way it was relaxing, knowing what to expect. Ms. P. S. gave a lot of quizzes, was fussy about neatness, and assigned a lot of oral reports. But she hardly ever gave detentions, she listened to excuses, and she never yelled. When she wanted to get the class's attention, she let her voice get quieter and quieter, until you almost had to read her lips.

Mary Ellen took a look at the quiz. Good, a review of fractions and decimals, an easy A. She did the problems quickly, then sat back to double-check her answers, admiring the neatness of her numbers. Ms. P. S. should be happy about that improvement over last year. Glancing across the aisle, Mary Ellen caught Ben looking at her curiously. Still humiliated, she swept her eyes past him, pretending to look out the window.

"All right, class. Time's up," Ms. P. S. announced. "Exchange papers with the person on your right and we'll correct them."

Justine was on Mary Ellen's right. They traded icy stares along with their papers. Ms. P. S. read off the answers and they switched back.

"Sixty percent?!" Mary Ellen yelped loudly. Math was her second best subject, right behind science.

"What's the problem, Mary Ellen?" Ms. P. S. walked down the aisle.

"She marked my paper wrong just because she's mad at me!" Seething, Mary Ellen handed her teacher the quiz, with Justine's big black X's next to four of the answers.

"I did not!" Justine said. She jumped out of her seat and pointed. "See, Ms. P. S.? That answer's supposed to be eleven. She has seventy-seven."

"It *is* eleven." Mary Ellen stood too. "Look. One, one." Mary Ellen jabbed the paper with her finger. She felt like jabbing Justine.

"Those don't look like ones to me. They have things on them. They look like sevens."

"Those aren't *things!* That's the real way to make a one—a little line on top and a little line on the bottom. And my sevens are slanted."

"Well, I couldn't tell the difference," Justine said snottily.

"Sit down, girls," Ms. P. S. said in a quiet voice. She looked closely at the paper. "Hmmm. All the answers marked wrong have either a one or a seven in them, Mary Ellen. It's very important to write clearly in math. I'm sorry, but I'm afraid I have to agree with Justine. You can take this grade, or you can stay after school and take a makeup quiz." Ms. P. S. walked back to her desk.

Justine made a face. Mary Ellen stuck out her tongue, then slumped down in her seat. She couldn't *wait* till Justine moved to Paris. The sooner the better. And good luck to all the Parisians, with such a two-faced back stabber in their midst!

"What's the matter with this family tonight?" Dr. Bobowick turned away from the meat loaf she was mixing and looked from her husband to Mary Ellen. "Why is everyone so disagreeable?"

Mary Ellen was at the table doing her homework.

"Well, how would you feel if you discovered that your best friend was a Benedict Arnold?" she said. "And you had to stay after school because she sabotaged your quiz grade?"

Mary Ellen's father put an innocent look on his face.

"All I said was, 'Why can't we have a normal vegetable instead of those oily red roots?'" He pointed to the bowl of sliced marinated beets on the counter. "Cucumbers, maybe. Or a salad. A salad would be nice."

"I hate those red roots. They stink!" Nicky looked up, grinning, from the kitchen desk, where he was pounding a Play-Doh snake into a Play-Doh pancake.

Dr. Bobowick frowned at her husband. "Thank you very much, Peter. Wonderful example. To answer your question, we are having beets tonight because the last of our lettuce bolted into bitter weedy stalks two weeks ago. Furthermore, because we have an organic garden, our cucumbers, without virtue of toxic pesticides, have fallen victim to *Acalymma vittata*, little striped beetles."

"I caught three striped beetles in a jar," Nicky said. "But they died. I forgot to make holes for the air."

"Leaving the jar in the sun didn't help," Mary Ellen said grouchily. "You roasted them. Poor little bugs."

"And Mary Ellen," Dr. Bobowick went on, "I know you're upset about Justine leaving, but I'd appreciate it if you'd stop moping around like you're ready to go out to our organic garden and eat worms."

"Do we have roganic worms?" Nicky asked. "Do roganic worms taste better than regular worms, Mommy?"

"Organic, sweetheart. And I was only kidding. We don't eat worms."

"I ate a caterpillar once."

"I remember." Dr. Bobowick pressed her lips together to keep from smiling.

"Fine. Beets are fine," Mr. Bobowick said in his phony tone, the one he used when he meant the exact opposite of what he was saying.

"Beets stink," Nicky announced. "I want roganic worms for dinner."

"Beets are yummy and good for you, Nicky," his mother said. "And they're your favorite color, red."

"I hate red," Nicky said cheerfully.

Mr. Bobowick held up the financial section of the evening paper. He hid behind it, talking to himself, but loud enough for everyone to hear:

"A man battles the bulls and bears of the stock market all day and he wants a little salad. He doesn't specify organic salad. Just a plain ordinary salad—"

He lowered the paper and peered over the top at Mary Ellen's mother, who was nodding as if she understood something now.

"Was the stock market down today, dear?" she asked.

"Thirty points." Mr. Bobowick shook his head sadly. "And another thing. Bananas. Just because we don't live in the tropics and grow our own bananas ... Of course, if the stock market did what a stock market should, maybe we could buy a vacation home on some nice little tropical island and then I could treat myself to an occasional homegrown banana."

Dr. Bobowick threw her hands in the air. "All right, all right. I get the message. Peter, you get an Academy Award for that magnificent performance. Mary Ellen, would you please take your bike to the Farmers' Market and get some lettuce and bananas for your poor malnourished father?" She took a bill from her purse and held it out to Mary Ellen.

Mr. Bobowick grinned, set down the paper, crossed the room, and kissed his wife. "You're a true gem, Laura."

Dr. Bobowick rolled her eyes. Mary Ellen grinned. Except for the glasses and the bald spot, her father looked just like Nicky when he got his own way.

Outside, as Mary Ellen rode past the Kellys' house, she saw Mrs. Kelly struggling to carry several pieces of matching luggage from their station wagon to the front door. The price tags were still on the handles. Mrs. Kelly looked like she could use a hand. Even though she was furious at Justine, Mary Ellen wasn't mad at the rest of the Kelly family. She slowed down.

"Hi, Mrs. Kelly."

"Oh, hello, Mary Ellen." Mrs. Kelly sounded a little out of breath, but she laughed lightly. "Can't go to Paris with ratty old suitcases, can we?"

Just on the verge of hopping off her bike, Mary Ellen stiffened. Paris again!

"No, I guess you can't, Mrs. Kelly," she said frostily, sped up, and rode on.

A string of small bells jingled when she pushed open the door to the Farmers' Market. Mr. Ellsworth was at the register counting money. "Getting ready to close up here, Mary Ellen."

"I only need lettuce and bananas, Mr. Ellsworth." She hurried to the shelf on the far wall and plucked a head of iceberg lettuce, then headed for the fruit racks. The bananas were swarming with fruit flies. Wrinkling her nose, she chose one of the greener bunches.

"You sure have a lot of fruit flies, Mr. Ellsworth," Mary Ellen commented, as the store owner weighed the bananas.

"Don't I know it! Always bad this time of year. Dadblasted pests!" He rang up the sale and took her money, shaking his head in disgust.

"Biologists do a lot of research on them," Mary Ellen told him. "My mother did her doctoral dissertation on fruit flies."

"Is that a fact? Well, I'm glad to hear they're good for something. Ask your mother if she wants to adopt some of mine."

Mary Ellen smiled politely, picked up the brown paper bag, and left the store. As she got on her bike, an idea blinked into her brain. Fruit flies. Biologists. Career Day. A great idea!

"Enjoy your TV dinners, guys," Mary Ellen told her fish. She shaved the chunk of frozen brine shrimp into the tank, as she did every night. Turning away from the aquarium, she caught a glimpse of Justine in the bedroom across the driveway.

Justine didn't look excited. In fact, she looked almost depressed. And she was chewing on the ends of her hair, which Mary Ellen hadn't seen her do in two years. Without warning Justine swung around and looked out her window. Their eyes met.

It sparked a memory for Mary Ellen, when they'd both had chicken pox in fourth grade. Their mothers had rigged up a plastic pail on a clothesline between the two bedrooms, so they could share books and treats and send notes back and forth while they were sick. The hook for the clothesline was still there, outside Mary Ellen's windowsill. But the special connection was gone.

Forget it. You should see her room—a total pigsty. The stinging words echoed in Mary Ellen's mind.

"So if you think it's that bad, then don't go looking in my room, you—you—" What was that French word for people who go around spying in other people's windows? "You voyeur!" Mary Ellen shouted through the open window, then angrily yanked the string that closed the blinds.

4 · FRUIT FLIES

Ms. P. S. stood on tiptoe and clapped her hands for attention. "All right now, everyone, take your seats."

The class was noisy and no one paid attention right away. The door to the adjoining classroom opened, and Miss Trink, the other sixth-grade teacher, poked her pointy nose in.

"Excuse me," she said in her high, shrill voice, frowning at Ms. P. S. like she was one of the kids. "We are *trying* to concentrate, and the din is disturbing us!" She gave her head a shake so her gray curls jiggled, then closed the door, catching part of her enormous flowy tent dress in it. Everyone started laughing. A second later the door opened again. This time, Miss Trink stood there with her arms folded until the class was silent. She gave Ms. P. S. a cranky look, then reclosed the door.

"Let's try not to disturb Miss Trink today," Ms. P. S. whispered.

Mary Ellen felt sorry for the kids who were stuck with the other sixth-grade teacher. Just having to listen to her voice all day long would be torture. She reached under her chair to make sure her Career Day exhibit was safe inside its brown paper bag, then scanned the room, carefully avoiding looking at Justine. They hadn't walked to school together that morning like they always did, because Mary Ellen had left early. It was probably just as well, since they weren't speaking to each other.

"Ms. P. S., Jason said he's going to pick one of my space-tomatoes and feed it to his dog to see if it will mutate," Debra called out.

"Well, I can't feed him any of mine, because I don't have any. My space-plant croaked," Jason said with a phony innocent grin.

"No one is going to eat anybody's tomatoes, Debra. Jason, get back to your seat."

"Would eating them really make a dog mutate?" Ben asked.

Ms. P. S. smiled. "No, I don't think there's any danger of that. Would someone like to explain our science project to Ben, since he wasn't here last year when we did Part One?"

"I will!" Jason turned around in his seat without waiting for Ms. P. S. to call on him. "See, we got these tomato seeds from NASA—all these fifth grades all over the whole country did—that NASA sent up into space so they'd get nuked by the sun."

"Radiated by the sun's rays," Ms. P. S. corrected. "Sometimes radiating seeds can cause a mutation in the plant. Can someone give an example?"

Mary Ellen's hand shot up.

"Mary Ellen?"

"Red grapefruit. They developed from white grapefruit seeds that were radiated."

"Very good." Ms. P. S. nodded and Mary Ellen smiled. She'd taken the experiment more seriously than anyone else in the class.

"So anyway," Jason went on, "We planted them and—"

"Don't forget about the control group," Mary Ellen cut in. "We planted regular seeds, too, the same kind, so we could compare things like height and when they flowered and got fruit and—"

"I was getting to that. Anyway, we got to take them home. It was no big deal. Nobody grew blue tomatoes, or anything."

"And we got to eat the regular ones," Kevin Middendorf said.

"We sent all our data to NASA, to be compiled with the results of the other schools that participated," Ms. P. S. explained. "Since we're all together again this year, I thought it would be interesting to harvest the seeds and follow the development through a second generation."

Mary Ellen looked over at the experiments that had made it through the summer. Out of the seventeen plants lined up along the windowsill, ranging from scraggly to sturdy, hers was definitely the healthiest looking. It had three plump, nearly ripe tomatoes on it. She cast a sideways glance at Ben. He seemed really interested.

"Now, we have a lot of Career Day reports to get through, so let's settle down," Ms. P. S. said.

Mary Ellen patted her exhibit again, feeling a little smug. The great idea she'd come up with yesterday was a live display to go with her career report. On her way to school this morning, she'd taken a detour by the Farmers' Market. She was equipped with a clean, extra-large mayonnaise jar, a piece of cloth cut from panty hose, and a thick rubber band. She caught Mr. Ellsworth just as he was getting ready to throw away a bin of mushy cherry tomatoes.

"Mr. Ellsworth, can I buy those?" she asked him.

"What, these rotten tomatoes? You don't want these, Mary Ellen. I'm getting a fresh batch in this afternoon. Why don't you come back—"

"No, I want those," Mary Ellen interrupted anxiously. "I want to adopt some fruit flies, for a project for school."

Mr. Ellsworth looked as if he thought she'd gone fruitier than the fruit flies, but he let her scoop some tomatoes into her jar.

"How much, Mr. Ellsworth?" she asked.

He scratched his head, then waved his hand. "On the house. I wouldn't know what to charge for rotten tomatoes and bugs."

Now Jason was eyeballing the bag. "Hey, Toothpick, what's in there?"

"None of your business, Metal-Mouth." Mary Ellen stuck out her tongue.

"Class.... Boys ... and ... girls.... Quiet....

Now." Ms. P. S.'s voice was dropping lower and lower.

When the only sounds in the classroom were creaking desks and kids breathing, Ms. P. S. smiled and started talking normally again.

"All right. Now for our Career Day reports. Ben Aldrich, why don't you go first?"

Mary Ellen could see that Ben was blushing even under his tan, as he shuffled to the front of the room. He was holding a videotape of an action movie.

"When I grow up, I want to move back to California and be a movie stuntman," he mumbled.

"Louder, please, Ben," Ms. P. S. said.

"A stuntman has to …" He was talking louder but looking at his shoes. He seemed so uncomfortable that it made Mary Ellen uncomfortable for him, so she looked away, staring out the window.

All the classroom windows were open, and dusty sunlight slanted in between the space-tomato plants. It was one of those mild September days when the air seems to hum. The autumn sky was pale blue. In nine days, Justine would be on a jumbo jet, up in that sky, headed more than five thousand miles away. Mary Ellen had measured it in the atlas.

Something nudged her elbow. Looking down, she saw a folded note that Justine had slipped onto her desk from across the aisle.

"'He's soooooo cute! You are so lucky you'll be sitting next to him all year!!! Luv, J.'" Mary Ellen read. She knew this was a peace offering, a chance to make up. She hesitated, feeling Justine's eyes on her.

Those don't look like ones to me. They have things on them.... You should see her room.

Mary Ellen sniffed, crumpled the paper, and stuck it in her desk. Forget it. With friends like that, who needs enemies? Out of the corner of her eye, she caught Justine's shrug and could almost hear her thinking, "So, fine for you. I'll have plenty of new friends in *Paris.*" Go ahead, Mary Ellen thought. Good riddance.

"And in my spare time, I want to be a world-class surfing champion." Ben was finishing his report.

"Very good, Ben," Ms. P. S. said. "You've given us a real idea of what a career as a stuntman would be like. I hope you have a good health insurance policy."

She smiled and nodded at Ben, who hurried back to his seat with his head down.

"Justine Kelly, next report please."

As Justine hopped up from her seat and scurried to the front of the room, Mary Ellen fixed a bored look on her face.

"I want to be a translator for the United Nations when I grow up." Justine taped a poster of the UN building onto the blackboard, set a French-English dictionary on the chalk ledge, and put on the headphones from her tape player. Everyone but Mary Ellen laughed. She started filling a dent in her desk with her pencil, trying not to listen.

"Going to Paris will be very good preparation for my chosen career. I'll be able to consolidate my second language early ..."

Consolidate her second language! She sounded like one of those magazine ads: *You, Too, Can Speak Ancient Egyptian in Only Thirty Days!* And what a coincidence that she just happened to work *Paris* into her report. Mary Ellen shook her head in disgust. What an attention-hog. Mary Ellen hoped she'd stay in France forever and wind up stuck in a cookie factory over there, writing stupid fortunes in French: *Beware of hairdressers who give you ze perm so you look like ze poodle.*

"Mary Ellen, are you with us today?" Ms. P. S.

startled Mary Ellen out of her daydream. Justine was back in her seat. Quickly, Mary Ellen grabbed the brown paper bag from under her seat and headed for the front of the room.

"I want to be a biologist when I grow up," Mary Ellen began, clutching the bag and staring at the floor.

"I don't think everyone can hear you, Mary Ellen," Ms. P. S. said.

Murmurs of, "No, we can't. Talk louder," echoed from the corners of the room. One of the voices was Justine's. Mary Ellen forced herself to hold her head up.

"I said I'm going to be a biologist," she shouted. "Can everyone hear me now?"

"I'm sure they can, Mary Ellen." Ms. P. S. winced at the volume. "But perhaps you can find a happy medium. Please go on."

"*Bios* is Greek for 'life' and *ologist* means 'one who studies.' A biologist is a scientist who studies life." So there. Let Justine talk French until her tongue fell off. Scientists had to know Greek and Latin and much harder stuff. "Some biologists study plants and some study animals. Some even study …" She paused, pulling the jar out of the bag. "Bugs! These are fruit flies. My mother did her thesis for her doctoral degree on fruit flies."

"That's fascinating, Mary Ellen." Ms. P. S. drew back a little nervously from the jar. "Would you like to pass them around for everyone to see?"

"Uh, sure, I guess so." She walked over to the first desk in the first row and handed the jar to Amy, trying not to smirk as Amy made a gagging face and quickly passed the jar behind her to Jason.

"Man, it's crawling with them. Hey, anyone want some spaghetti sauce à la bug?"

"Pass them back, Jason," Ms. P. S. said.

"The scientific name for fruit flies is *Drosophila.* Usually people think of fruit flies as pests, and they are in some ways. They eat a lot of fruit, and they really bug farmers."

Everyone chuckled and Mary Ellen straightened her shoulders, pleased with her accidental pun.

"But fruit flies are good for biological research because they multiply very fast. So biologists can study genetics because there's a whole new generation about once a month."

Mary Ellen could tell she was talking too fast, so she took a deep breath and tried to slow down. "One of the reasons biologists study fruit flies is to find out things about genes and DNA that might help find the cause of birth defects or diseases. Fruit flies lay their eggs in fruit—they eat fruit, and so do their larvae."

"Ugh. Larvae. Disgusting." Mary Ellen saw Justine shudder, and she grinned wickedly.

"Lots and lots of larvae," she repeated. "Fruit flies especially like to lay their eggs and hatch their *larvae* in tomatoes, apples, oranges, bananas, and …" She tried to think which fruits at the market were the worst. "And, um, pineapples and kiwis. And melons. They love melons."

The jar was making its way around the room, and Mary Ellen noticed that Ben held onto it for a long time and seemed really curious.

"If you're a scientist and you want to do research, you can even buy instant fruit flies. Well, not exactly instant—it's *larvae* in this mushy stuff in a test tube. They take about ten days to hatch. There's all different brands—I mean, kinds—thousands."

"Are yours instant?" Ben asked.

Mary Ellen shook her head. "Mine are wild fruit flies. I captured them at the Farmers' Market this morning. Anyway, I think a career as a biologist would be really neat." She turned and smiled at Ms. P. S.

"Well, that's very interesting, Mary Ellen. Thank you." She handed Mary Ellen the jar, which the last student in the last row had brought up to her desk. "It's a wonderful *science* report," she said, with a gentle emphasis on science.

Mary Ellen stared blankly at her. Science report? It wasn't a science report.

"I wish you'd said a little less about larvae, though, and a little more about why you want to be a biologist and what biologists do. This was an assignment on careers."

With a sinking feeling in her stomach, Mary Ellen detected Ms. P. S.'s good-try-but-B-minus tone of voice. Her great idea was a flop.

Clutching the jar, she could feel her face burning as she moved back toward her seat.

"Hey, Toothpick, do fruit flies like strawberries?" Jason whispered, as she passed his desk.

Mary Ellen held her head up stiffly, not looking at anyone. What happened next seemed to happen in slow motion. At one moment, Mary Ellen was a few feet away from her desk. The next, her foot was catching on something. Stumbling, she let go of the jar. Her knee hit the floor with a hot stinging skid, and the jar flew at the cinder-block back wall and shattered.

Stunned, Mary Ellen knelt back and rubbed her smarting knee.

"*Eeee-ew!* LARVAE!" Justine squealed.

"Very smooth, Toothpick!" Jason started clapping. Everyone in the class was howling with laughter.

"Don't anyone move!" Ms. P. S. was actually shouting over the uproar. "Kevin, please go find Mr. George. Tell him we've had an accident, and ask him if he can come to clean it up right away." Ms. P. S. tiptoed toward Mary Ellen, trying to avoid the broken glass. "Mary Ellen, are you all right?"

Mary Ellen nodded dumbly and stood. For some reason, an expression her father always used when he paid the bills popped into her head: *If it weren't for bad luck, I'd have no luck at all!*

She saw Ms. P. S. looking at the small black swarm of fruit flies that was spreading out from the pulpy tomato mess. A few of the boldest bugs were beginning to make a beeline—or a fruit-fly line—toward the seventeen space-tomato plants.

"What exactly did you say about how rapidly fruit flies multiply, Mary Ellen?" whispered Ms. P. S.

5 · FISH, FRIENDS & FAMILIES

"Hey, you big bully, get away from him!" Mary Ellen tapped on the aquarium glass, scolding the larger of her two striped damselfish as it chased the gold-tail blue away from a shred of shrimp.

She opened her lab notebook.

Sunday, September 17
    A. Observations
        a. When fish get stressed out, their gills pump faster. Like rapid breathing, I guess.
        b. The big black-and-white one always

picks on the blue-and-gold one.

    c. I don't think the blue-and-gold is getting enough to eat. He looks kind of skinny and pale—not as blue as he used to be.

  B. Questions

Mary Ellen chewed on the tip of her pen for a minute, watched the bolder fish chase the timid one under a rock, then started writing again.

    a. Can someone get picked on to death?
    b. Are fish as mean as kids?

Slowly Mary Ellen closed the notebook and let it drop to the floor. She felt like the blue-and-gold fish.

The past week had to go on record as the most miserable week of her life. On the way out of school after the disastrous Career Day report, Mary Ellen was lagging to one side of the hallway, waiting for the regular group of walkers, clustered on the front steps of the building, to leave. The doors were open and she could hear Amy and Debra fawning all over Justine, talking French fashions and makeup, while Jason made cracks about learning the cancan.

On his way out of the building, Ben spotted Mary Ellen and paused, kind of shyly.

"Hey, those bugs were pretty cool," he said. "That was a good idea. Fruit flies. How'd you think of it?"

Mary Ellen had almost smiled, but she remembered his "dots" comment just in time, and scowled instead. She brushed by him without a word and almost bumped smack into Justine, who was closest to the door.

"Maybe it's because her little brother calls her 'Melon,'" Justine giggled to Ben.

"Hey, we should call her Mary Melon," Kevin Middendorf squeaked.

Mary Ellen gritted her teeth and kept walking. Unbelievable. Even old Peanut-Butter-and-Pickle-Breath had turned against her.

Jason took up the chant. "Mary Melon. No, I got it! Hairy Melon. Hairy Melon and Her Famous Fruit Flies."

"It'll blow over," Dr. Bobowick had said that night. "These things do. They'll forget all about it."

But it didn't. Not the next day. Or the next. No one forgot about it because the fruit flies had settled into their new space-tomato homes like they were fruit-fly condos. All day long, little black specks floated around. All day long, kids swiped at them. The fruit flies flew in lazy loops, always managing to swoop out of reach just as someone grabbed the air for them.

They harvested the seeds from three of the plants Friday morning, but that left fourteen to go. To make matters worse, the bugs had spread— they had migrated through the door to Miss Trink's classroom. Miss Trink didn't have space-tomatoes, but her whole room was like a green-house: African violets, begonias, spider plants, ferns. And her special pets—miniature citrus trees.

"An infestation!" Miss Trink complained to Ms. P. S. "My oranges will be ravaged! My lemons are in danger of being decimated!"

They couldn't use regular pesticides inside the school. Miss Trink had tried spraying garlic water on the plants, but the only noticeable effect was to make both classrooms smell like a pizza parlor.

"We're all going to smell like garlic at my party tonight, and it's your fault, Mary Ellen," Amy said loudly at the end of the day. It was a boy-girl party, at the bowling alley, and all the girls who were invited were going over to Amy's house, then on to the bowling alley together. Justine was invited this year. Mary Ellen wasn't.

Justine looked away when Amy said that, as if she felt guilty. Well, she should.

"Have a great time," Mary Ellen said as sarcastically as she could, on her way out of school. "I hope you drop a bowling ball on your toe."

Justine hadn't answered.

"Can I help you feed your fish, Melon?" Nicky pranced into the room, breaking into Mary Ellen's stream of gloomy thoughts. "Me and Dizzy wanna help."

Melon! Ouch! Well, at least she wasn't Toothpick anymore. "I already fed them, Nicky."

"How 'bout their dessert? Did they have their dessert yet? Can I give it to them?" he persisted. "Please?"

"We-lll, okay. Just a tiny bit. You can't feed them too much, or they get stomachaches. Here, hold out your hand." Mary Ellen poured a few flakes into his palm, then held him up and lifted the tank cover so he could dump them in.

This time, the blue-and-gold managed to bolt down a few morsels before getting chased away. Because the others were already full and didn't want them, Mary Ellen thought. *You pigs! You bul-*

lies! She was really starting to identify with the underfish.

"What's their names?" Nicky asked.

"I haven't named them yet," Mary Ellen admitted. She probably should. After all, they were pets, too, not just biological specimens. "Want to help me?"

"Sure." Nicky screwed up his face in thought. "The black-and-white one could be Tiger. Tigers have stripes."

"But tigers are orange-and-black striped. How about Zebra?" Mary Ellen said.

"Uh-uh. I saw it on TV. It was a tiger, white and black. Really."

"Okay, Tiger's fine," Mary Ellen said. It didn't matter that much. And anyway, tigers were much meaner than zebras. "And we can call the smaller striped one Tiger Too. And the blue one with the gold tail, he's the underdog, so I think I'll call him Underfish."

"Like Underdog in the cartoon?"

"No. The underdog is the weakest one, the one you don't think is going to win, like in football, or in elections."

"Oh." Nicky's head was moving back and forth

in front of the tank, as he gazed at the fish.

"What about the blue one?" Mary Ellen asked.

"Maybe Dizzy," Nicky suggested.

"But we already have one Dizzy in the house. That might get confusing."

"How about Lizzy?" He turned around and looked at Mary Ellen seriously.

"Hmmm. I don't know." Mary Ellen hid a smile.

"Izzy? Grizzy? Tizzy?"

Now Mary Ellen couldn't help grinning. "Maybe we should think about that one."

Nicky turned back to the fish tank to watch Tiger harass Underfish. Across the driveways, the lights in Justine's room blinked on. Quickly, Mary Ellen turned her back to the window.

"Melon?"

"What, Nicky?" Mary Ellen answered absently.

"What makes the bubbles?"

"An air pump." Mary Ellen picked up her backpack from the floor and put it on her bed. They were having an English test tomorrow. If she and Justine were still friends, they'd probably be studying together. Maybe it was just as well they weren't. The sooner she got used to being friend-less, the better. It was weird. Even though she hated Justine now, she still kind of missed her. There was a sort of hole in her days where Justine used to be. She snuck a peek at Justine's room, but the light was off again. Soon the whole house would be empty, which was exactly how Mary Ellen felt. And alone. Like a single amoeba on a microscope slide.

"Melon?"

"What, Nicky?"

"Why are there bubbles in the fish tank?"

"It's to mix the water up and provide more surface area for the interchange of gases—oxygen and carbon dioxide."

"Hunh?" Nicky looked confused.

"It helps the fish breathe."

"But fish don't breathe. They drink. And swim."

"Yes, they do breathe. See those little curved things behind their heads? Those are gills. That's how fish breathe."

"When I tried to breathe in the bathtub, I got water up my nose. It didn't feel good."

"That's because humans don't have gills," Mary Ellen told him.

"Oh." Nicky stared hard at the tank. "The fish need those bubbles?"

"Yep." Mary Ellen frowned a little as she noticed a patch of algae on one side of the tank, a patch she'd missed when she cleaned the tank last week. "I have to clean this tank again."

"Now? Can I help you?"

"No, not now. Maybe tomorrow. I have studying to do." Mary Ellen looked around her room. The disarray was worse than usual. "I can't study in here. I'm going downstairs. Come on, Nicky."

"Can I stay and watch the fish? Please?"

"Well, okay. Just don't touch anything." Mary Ellen unzipped her backpack, took out her English book, and trudged down to the kitchen.

Her mother was sitting at the table with her grandmother.

"Oh, hi, Gram. I didn't know you were here." Mary Ellen leaned down to kiss her cheek, and noticed an elastic bandage wrapped around Gram's left wrist. "What happened?"

"Three guesses, and the first two don't count," Dr. Bobowick said dryly.

"Karate?"

Gram looked embarrassed.

"Sprained it doing handstands."

"Handstands?" Mary Ellen looked at her

mother, then back at Gram. "That's gymnastics."

"It's one of our karate exercises too. It's supposed to strengthen the arms." Gram grimaced slightly. "It makes me so mad I could spit tacks. Here I am, doing my best to build this old body up, and it lets me down."

"Karate's a sport that puts a strain on even young and conditioned athletes, Mother," Dr. Bobowick said gently. "Don't you think you could build your body up with a less rigorous sport?"

"Well, I guess I don't have a choice, do I?"

Mary Ellen watched as her mother and grandmother locked gazes, just like the staring contests she and Justine used to have. Dr. Bobowick won.

Gram looked away and chuckled, a little bitterly. "I know, I know. Shall I take up croquet?" she asked in a high-pitched la-di-da voice.

"I doubt you could play croquet with that wrist," Dr. Bobowick said mildly.

Gram sighed. Mary Ellen felt bad for her.

"Couldn't you still do the karate when your arm gets better, but just take it easier?" she asked.

"Oh, that's probably what I'll do, Mary Ellen. It's the reasonable thing, I suppose. Although I've never been the world's most reasonable woman.

Don't see why I should have to start now."

"In biology it's called adaptation, Mother," Dr. Bobowick said. She smiled.

"So all right. I'll adapt." Gram sat back in her chair and adjusted her glasses, then peered sharply at Mary Ellen. "Your mother tells me the Kellys are moving. Speaking of adapting, how are you adapting to the prospect of your best friend flitting off to France for a year?"

"Best friend? Ha!" Mary Ellen snorted. She sat down next to her mother, put her homework stuff on the table, and started pulling a long thread from the fringe of a place mat.

"Not getting along?" Gram inquired.

"I'm getting along fine. Justine's the one who's turned into a back-stabbing two-faced snot. Ever since she found out she's going to Paris, her head's so big she's going to need a size three hundred beret."

Glancing up from the place mat, Mary Ellen caught her mother and grandmother exchanging smiles. "What?" she said. "What are you smiling about?"

"If I recall correctly, Laura, some of the worst fights we ever had were right before you went away somewhere. Back to college after vacations, the year you studied in Grenada."

"Mmmm." Mary Ellen's mother was nodding. "True. It's hard to say good-bye sometimes. Sometimes it's easier just to get mad and go your separate ways. It doesn't seem to hurt as much. On the surface anyway."

"Is this a lecture in disguise?" Mary Ellen asked.

Gram and her mother both chuckled.

Taking the string she'd unwoven from the place mat, Mary Ellen tied the two ends together and wound it around her fingers, making a miniature cat's cradle. She and Justine used to play that game all the time. They used to play all the time, period. And fight, once in a while, but never stay mad at each other like this. Mary Ellen knew she'd been the one who started it, being so mean about Paris. All of a sudden she felt the week's worth of anger subside. She missed Justine. Missed her already, and she wasn't even gone yet. But she would be in five more days.

"Should I call her?"

Dr. Bobowick lifted her shoulders in a slight shrug. Gram did the same. Neither said a word.

Mary Ellen dropped the string, stood, and walked over to the phone to call before she could change her mind. It rang as she reached for the receiver.

"Hello?" she said quickly, anxious to get rid of whoever it was, so she could get the hard part over with.

"Mary Ellen?" It was Justine. Her voice was thick, like she either had a cold or had been crying. "Listen, I know you're mad at me, but I have a present for you. Like a reverse going-away present."

"I'm not mad at you," Mary Ellen cut in. "Well, I was. But not really. It's complicated. Anyway, I'm sorry I've been acting like such a jerk."

"Can you come over? I'm still packing."

Mary Ellen looked at her mother. "Is it all right if I go—"

"Go." Dr. Bobowick waved her hand.

"I'll be right there," she said, and hung up.

6 · CRYSTALS & BUBBLES

"A necklace. It's beautiful!" Mary Ellen gazed at the blackish crystal pendant in her palm. It was about an inch long, with one end of the stone encased in a silver cup with a ring for the chain; the other came to three jagged points. She ran her finger lightly over the grooves in the surface.

"Hold it up to the light," Justine said.

Mary Ellen picked up the silver chain and let the crystal dangle in front of the lamp on Justine's night table. The light revealed dark green translucent spots in the stone.

"It's a power crystal," Justine told her. "Olivia

helped me pick it out at the New Age Cave downtown."

"What does it do?" Mary Ellen put the chain around her neck. "Here, help me put it on."

"Hold up your hair." Justine fastened the clasp. "Power crystals are supposed to tap into forces in the earth, or something, and transfer them to you. You have to meditate on it every day and picture what you want to happen."

"I wonder what would happen if I pictured you staying home instead of going to Paris." Mary Ellen fingered the pendant. "I'm only kidding," she added, as Justine's face fell. "I'm glad for you. Really." But she couldn't help sighing. "I'm just sad for me."

"You know, I don't really want to go that much," Justine said slowly. "I mean, I sort of do, because it'll be interesting and all. But I won't know anyone. I won't even know how to talk. What if I go into a restaurant and order something like fried pig brains or frog's eggs by mistake?"

"School's going to be the worst for me. Jason has everyone calling me Hairy Melon." Mary Ellen flopped on Justine's bed. She saw Justine eye her shoes on the bedspread, and shifted her legs, hanging her feet over the side.

"Jason wouldn't have said that if I hadn't blabbed about Nicky calling you Melon," said Justine. "I'm sorry."

"Well, it's better than Toothpick, I guess."

"He's so disgusting. You know what he gave Amy for her birthday? That horrible slimy stuff that comes in the plastic mushroom, Funny Fungus."

"She deserves it," Mary Ellen said. "How can you stand hanging around with her, anyway?"

Justine shrugged and started stacking books from her bookshelf neatly in a cardboard carton. "You were mad at me. I really don't like her at all. You should have seen her at the bowling alley. She put her fingers in the bowling ball and when she rolled it, one of her fingernails came off."

"Ouch!"

Justine was shaking her head and giggling. "No, they're those fake kind, the ones you glue on. And underneath, hers were bitten worse than yours!"

Mary Ellen grinned.

"And she was clinging to Ben like—like ivy. Poison ivy." Justine stood up and imitated Amy, drawing back her arm, and dropping an imaginary bowling ball behind her. "'Oh, it's so-oo heavy.

Ben, can you help me?' She even sat on his lap!"

"Weren't her parents there? What did they say? What did Ben say?"

"Her mother was getting the food. And Amy pretended it was an accident. Ben was sitting on the bench and she just backed up like she was totally exhausted from bowling, and sat down on him like he was a piece of furniture. And she knows I have a crush on him too. Not that it makes any difference. I won't be around to do anything about it."

So Justine had had a lousy time at the party. Mary Ellen couldn't help feeling a little twinge of satisfaction. But now Justine was looking depressed again.

"Tell me more about my necklace," Mary Ellen said, changing the subject.

"It's a tourmaline. Different crystals are supposed to work on different things, like happiness or inner peace. This one is for getting rid of negative energy. You know, like bad luck."

"Did you buy it because of the mirror?"

"Well, I figured crystal power was probably as real as broken-mirror bad luck. And it was partly my fault about the mirror." Justine put her hand over her mouth, hiding a smile. "That really was bad luck with the fruit flies."

They looked at each other and burst out laughing.

"Did you see the look on Ms. P. S.'s face when she saw them head for the space-tomatoes?" Justine did a perfect imitation of their teacher's expression.

"And Miss Trink, spraying all that garlic water, like she was trying to ward off vampires instead of bugs!"

"Justine, are you packing?" Mr. Kelly's booming voice asked from the hall.

"Yes, Daddy," Justine called back sweetly, then wrinkled her nose. "He's been so cranky this week. Last night he and Olivia had a huge fight about him wanting her to get a pair of decent shoes."

"Why would Olivia get mad because he wants to buy her new shoes?"

"Decent shoes. The key word is decent. Could you hand me that koala bear?"

Mary Ellen reached behind her head, pulled out the stuffed animal, and tossed it to Justine, who tucked it into another box.

"Olivia said no way will she wear leather,

because it's immoral for vegetarians," Justine went on. "And then Daddy said no way will he let her wear ratty old sneakers in first class."

"You're flying first class?"

Justine nodded. "Daddy has such long legs and he needs a seat with lots of room."

"So who won the shoe fight?"

"It was a tie. Mom went out and bought Olivia a pair of those flat cotton shoes with straps and embroidery on the toes."

"Justine, as soon as you're finished in there, get down to the kitchen and help your mother."

Mary Ellen raised her eyebrows. Mr. Kelly did sound awfully cranky. Justine made a face in the direction of the door.

"Want me to help?" Mary Ellen asked sympathetically.

"That's okay. I'm almost done."

Mary Ellen looked around the room. Boxes were lined up neatly against one wall, filled with all of Justine's stuff, her porcelain-dog collection, her stuffed animals, her books. All the posters had already been taken down and were rolled up with rubber bands.

"I can't believe you're going," Mary Ellen said. "I'm really going to miss you."

"I'm going to miss you too. I'm even going to miss your messy room."

"You are?"

"Yeah, it's kind of relaxing to hang out in. As long as I don't have to—"

Mary Ellen laughed and finished for her. "It's a nice place to visit, but you wouldn't want to live there."

"Like Paris, maybe." Justine sighed. "It's starting to hit me now. We're actually going. I think I liked the idea of it a lot better than I'm going to like doing it, you know?"

"Are you bringing all your stuff with you?"

Justine shook her head. "Hardly anything. We'll be renting a furnished apartment. Most of our stuff's going into storage for the year. The movers will be here Thursday."

"Thursday? I thought you weren't leaving till Friday," Mary Ellen said, dismayed. A day less than she'd thought.

"Our flight's on Friday," Justine explained. "Thursday's my last day at school. We're going to stay downtown at the New England Inn that night because there won't be any sheets or anything. I hate that someone's renting our house. Some stranger's going to be sleeping in my bed.

Eeee-ew! But at least we're having dinner at your house."

"My mother invited you to dinner?" She hadn't said anything to Mary Ellen. Maybe she'd been waiting to see if Mary Ellen and Justine made up.

"Hey, could you ask her to make her lemon-ginger chicken? I really love that."

Mary Ellen nodded, then stood up. "Well, I better let you finish packing," she said glumly.

Justine pulled a lock of hair across her mouth, started to chew it, then spit it out. "Ugh. I can't believe I'm doing that again. I need to take a break. I'll walk you halfway."

Neither one said anything as they went downstairs and outside.

"Thanks for the crystal." Mary Ellen stood on the Kellys' side of the hedge, holding it tightly. "I really love it."

"I hope it works. Don't forget the meditating part. Olivia says that's really important."

"Justine!" Mr. Kelly roared from somewhere in the house.

"Gotta go. See you tomorrow." Justine turned and hurried back inside.

Mary Ellen stood for a moment, then ducked through the hedge.

The kitchen was empty when she went in.

"Mom?"

"In here." Dr. Bobowick called from her study.

Mary Ellen poked her head through the open door, then stepped in. Her mother was working on a stack of quiz papers, grading the top one with a red felt-tip pen.

"Wrong…. Wrong…. Check. This is getting monotonous." Dr. Bobowick removed her reading glasses. "Are things all better?"

Mary Ellen nodded.

"Good."

Mary Ellen leaned down and showed her the pendant. "See what Justine gave me?"

"Very pretty, honey." Her mother smiled briefly, then put her glasses back on and turned back to the quizzes. "Wrong, wrong, wrong," she groaned.

Mary Ellen left the study and wandered into the den, where her father was sitting on the couch with Nicky. They were watching the news.

"Is it over yet, Dad?" Nicky asked.

"Not yet, Nicko." Mr. Bobowick kept watching the TV.

Mary Ellen wiggled herself in between Nicky and her father.

"Now, Dad? Is it over now?"

"Uh-uh. Not yet."

Mary Ellen waited what she considered a sufficient pause to space out the interruptions. "Dad?"

Mr. Bobowick tossed his hands up. "It's a conspiracy. You two want your father to be ignorant of current events. Which will be sad, because a stockbroker needs to know what's going on in the world or he might not make proper business decisions. In which case, his boss will fire him and he and his whole family will wind up living in the poorhouse."

"Is the poorhouse near Paris?" Nicky asked. "Are we gonna move, too, like the Kellys?"

Mr. Bobowick let his head drop against the back of the couch and groaned, but Mary Ellen could see he was trying not to smile.

"I give up. You win. No, Nicky, we're not moving." He switched the TV to the cable cartoon channel, and set the remote control on the coffee table.

Now Mr. Bobowick turned to Mary Ellen. "Yes, sweetheart, what can I do for you?" he asked with exaggerated politeness.

"I just wanted to show you my going-away present from Justine. See? It's a power crystal."

"A power crystal? Are we talking witchcraft? Or some new source of energy that might lower my electric bill?"

"Uh-uh. This one's supposed to ward off negative energy. There are all different kinds."

"Power crystals, eh? I've heard of power lunches and power neckties, but I don't think power crystals have reached the financial community yet. I wonder if there's one to make the stock market go the right way."

"There might be. One for good luck. Dad, do you believe in luck?"

"Luck, eh? The luck of the draw, the roll of the dice, the spin of giddy Fortune's furious fickle wheel—"

"But do you think it's real?" Mary Ellen cut in.

"Do I think luck is real?" Mr. Bobowick scratched his head. "Well, honey, if there's such a thing as luck in my line of work, I think it's probably the intersection of opportunity with preparation. I study the market, do my homework, keep my eyes open, and try to pounce on opportunities when I see them." He nodded seriously, then winked. "Of course, I wouldn't want to lose my lucky tie tack. Just in case."

Mary Ellen smiled.

"Well, since Nicky's taken over the TV, I think I'll go in the other room and try my luck with the newspaper." Mr. Bobowick pushed himself up off the couch.

Mary Ellen spread out in the space he vacated, and tuned in to Wile E. Coyote, watching him set a trap for the Roadrunner. Nicky's eyes were glued to the screen.

"So, did you think of a name for the blue fish yet?"she asked, nudging him with her toe. He didn't say anything. Mary Ellen reached over and shook his arm lightly. His sleeve was damp. "Anybody home in there?"

Nicky kept his eyes on the cartoon.

The cloud of dust that signaled the Roadrunner's approach was getting bigger.

"Melon, are you sure bubbles are good for your fish?" Nicky asked the question without turning his head.

"Sure I'm sure."

Wile E. was off the cliff now, with a sputtering rocket strapped to his back. He looked right at Mary Ellen, with an expression that seemed to say, "Not again!" Below him was a canyon, with the ground hundreds of feet down. There was a thin blue thread of river at the bottom.

An alarm went off in Mary Ellen's head. River—water—wet sleeve. She sniffed suspiciously. Lilacs. Grabbing Nicky's arm, she pulled it over to her nose. He squirmed and pulled away.

"What's that smell, Nicky?"

Nicky still didn't turn his head away from the television, but Mary Ellen knew he was listening by the nervous way he was blinking.

On the screen, Wile E. Coyote hit the bottom. SPLASH! Big-eyed Roadrunner grinned slyly. *Mbeep-mbeep!* And Mary Ellen figured out what the smell was. Bubble bath.

"Nicky? You didn't—" Panicking, Mary Ellen leapt off the couch and raced up to her room.

"NO-OOOOO-OOOOO!" she wailed, standing in the doorway.

Mary Ellen's desk chair was pulled in front of the aquarium. The lid was open and a mound of fine, fluffy, lilac-scented bubbles was bulging out the top and oozing down the front of the tank. The filter and the air pump were churning up more by the second.

"Mary Ellen, what's the matter?" Her mother raced down the hall, put her hands on Mary Ellen's shoulders, and spun her around. "Are you all right?"

"Look! Look what he did!" Her arm was shaking as she pointed to the fish tank.

Dr. Bobowick looked. A peculiar expression crossed her face. Then she sprang into action.

"Come on, let's get the net and see if we can save your fish."

Mary Ellen's father had come running, too, and now stood behind her mother.

"Peter, can you run out to the pet store and get a small tank? A ten-gallon one. You should have one anyway, Mary Ellen, in case you have to isolate sick fish."

"These fish aren't sick, they're poisoned! Where is that little menace? I'm gonna put *him* in the tank—"

Dr. Bobowick blocked Mary Ellen's way.

"Find Nicky and take him with you, would you, dear?" she said to her husband. "Come on, Mary Ellen. The net." She guided Mary Ellen over to the tank and rummaged in the cabinet beneath, pulling out the green-mesh net, and the box of sea salt. "Here, you go down and mix some new water in a bowl. I'll go fishing." She put the salt into Mary Ellen's hands and gave her a gentle shove. "Quick. New water."

As Mary Ellen hurried down the stairs, she

heard Nicky calling to her. "I helped you clean your tank, Melon. It smells better now too. Maybe you can name the blue fish Fizzy."

Mr. Bobowick took one look at Mary Ellen's face as she stormed into the kitchen, and hoisted Nicky up protectively. "We'll be right back."

"But Daddy, bubbles are good for fish," Nicky said as they went out the door. "Melon said so."

"Wrong kind of bubbles, Nicko," she heard her father reply.

Mary Ellen shivered as she scrounged in the cabinets for a big bowl. Bad luck: First, it attacked her. Now it was attacking her fish. Was bad luck contagious?

7 · FISH & FLU

Monday, September 18
    A. Observations
        a. Tank empty, rinsed, rinsed, and rinsed
          again. Soap-free (I hope).
    B. Equipment Needed:
        a. New crushed shell for bottom.
        b. New charcoal and white stuff for
          filter.
        c. New fish.
    C. Questions

Mary Ellen started to gnaw on her thumbnail.
"Ouch!" She pulled it away from her mouth.

After last week, all her nails were bitten down so far that they hurt. Maybe she'd try to quit again. She chewed on the end of her pen instead.

Questions. How about—if there was such a thing as luck, who was in charge of it, God? Somehow she couldn't picture God being so—so random. Or so mean, if there was anything to that superstitious stuff. Maybe God put someone else in charge of things like luck and weather, some joker with a personality like Jason Hodges. Were there any rules that the head of the luck department had to play by? Like, did the size of the broken mirror have anything to do with the size of the bad luck? Shouldn't breaking a small mirror mean only a small amount of bad luck? Would everything have turned out differently if *Justine* had picked the cookie with the REFLECT CAREFULLY fortune in it?

Questions. What questions could she have about an empty fish tank? Beneath her notes, Mary Ellen doodled a gravestone. Her father had dumped the deceased on the compost heap. Next spring they'd be pushing up the daisies. Or, more likely, zucchini or sugar snap peas or tomatoes. Gloomily she filled in the gravestone with an epitaph:

R.I.P.

TIGER, TIGER TOO, UNDERFISH, AND FIZZY
THEY WERE CUTE FISH WHO GAVE THEIR LIVES
FOR SCIENCE

It was an exaggeration, but Mary Ellen felt they deserved that, at least, after being bubbled to death.

Sighing, she closed the notebook, and let her pen drop. It landed on a pile of Monopoly money on the floor. She felt awful. Her head felt heavy and stuffy, like her sinuses were filled with cement. Her throat was scratchy. Dragging herself off the bed, she waded through dirty clothes and assorted bedroom debris over to the dresser, and stood there looking in the mirror.

The reflection of her room looked like something Lewis Carroll might have thought up if he'd been reading Stephen King. Her coral-reef poster was falling down and a corner was partially torn off. Desk drawers were open and the desk top was piled with a mountain of crumpled papers. Half her books weren't on their shelves, and the ones that were, were mostly sideways or backward.

"Ugh. What a mess." She stared at herself in the mirror. "And you. You're a mess. An ugly mess."

"Mary Ellen Bobowick, I hope you don't really feel that way about yourself." Dr. Bobowick stepped into the room, holding a basket full of clean, folded clothes.

"Yes, I do. Look at all these dots. Why did I have to be born with dot genes?"

Mary Ellen could see her mother trying not to smile. "I'm afraid you inherited those from me. Some people think those 'dots' are beautiful. Daddy always said that's what first attracted him to me. Freckles."

"Well, he's weird, then," Mary Ellen said grumpily. "No offense. Look at me. I look absolutely disgusting. My eyes are all puffy—"

"You were crying about your fish."

"And my nose is all red and stuffed up—"

"I repeat, you—"

"And I have soap scum and salt crud all over my clothes and my hair—"

"Nothing a shower won't cure." Dr. Bobowick frowned with concern. "And speaking of showers, what is this shower of negativity? I thought you felt much better about things since you and Justine made up."

"I did. But I don't anymore. I mean, I'm happy we're friends again and all, but she's going away, so what difference does it make? I feel horrible."

"You sound a little hoarse." Putting the laundry basket down, Mary Ellen's mother picked her way across the floor and placed a cool palm on Mary Ellen's forehead. "You feel warm too. Is your throat sore?"

Mary Ellen nodded.

"Open up. Let me see." Dr. Bobowick peered into Mary Ellen's mouth for a moment. "It's a bit red. I think you better get yourself to bed. If it doesn't feel better tomorrow, I'll take you for a strep test."

Dr. Bobowick looked at the bed, then shook her head, stepped over, and started clearing items off the tangled covers.

"What are all these rocks doing here?"

"It's my geological collection. I was examining them."

"Don't they go someplace?" Her mother stood there holding an oval piece of granite that Mary Ellen thought looked like an egg, and a flattish white-and-brown rock that she'd picked up at the beach because it reminded her of an English muffin.

"On that shelf." Mary Ellen pointed to the shorter of her two bookcases, which was draped with all the sweaters she'd pulled out of the box in her closet when she was looking for her yellow one.

Dr. Bobowick shook her head again and put the rocks on the floor near the foot of the bed. "I'm not a fanatic about neatness like Mrs. Kelly, Mary Ellen, but it looks to me like your room has gotten way out of hand. Maybe that's part of the reason you're depressed."

"I know. I'm a slob. An ugly, skinny slob, with dots." Mary Ellen flopped on the bed.

"You stop that, Mary Ellen," her mother said, wagging her finger for emphasis. "You are a beautiful, creative, intelligent young woman."

"Then why am I so—so—"

"Here, get under these covers." Dr. Bobowick pulled back the quilt, and Mary Ellen squirreled under them. "Honey, everyone goes through an awkward stage. It's part of the transition from being a cute little kid to being a full-fledged teenager. Think of yourself as being a diamond in the rough."

"I feel more like a chunk of gravel from the driveway," grumbled Mary Ellen, but she gave her mother a small smile.

Mr. Bobowick stopped at the door with Nicky clinging to his back, and caught her last comment.

"Don't you believe it, kiddo. You'll be a true gem, just like your mother. All you need is a little polish." He took a look around her room. "And maybe a housekeeping service. Are you sick, sweetheart?"

Mary Ellen nodded.

"A few people in my office are out with the flu. Early in the season for it. Well, Nicky, let's flee the flu." He swung Nicky around, held him out like Superman, and whizzed him down the hall, making airplane noises.

"I'll go get you something for the fever and to clear your stuffy nose." Mary Ellen's mother straightened out the covers and left the room.

Mary Ellen woke up immediately when the light went on. Her mother was standing next to the bed in a bathrobe and pajamas.

"What time is it?" she asked groggily.

"Eleven-thirty. Time for a second dose." Dr. Bobowick held out two pills and a tall glass of orange juice.

Mary Ellen sat up and swallowed the medicine.

Her mother fluffed up her pillow. "With plenty of rest and a little luck, maybe you'll be back in school by Wednesday or Thursday."

"Luck. Ha. If I have to count on my luck for anything, I'm in big trouble. It's just not fair, getting sick on top of everything else. And I *have* to go to school on Thursday. Our class is having a bon voyage party for Justine."

"Keep your voice, down, Mary Ellen, you'll wake Nicky."

"That little fishkiller—"

"Don't," her mother said softly. "Look. Or look-it, as Nicky would say." She pointed to the empty aquarium. Lying on the plastic filter bed was Dizzy the lizard.

"He didn't have to do that," Mary Ellen mumbled, feeling guilty about all the rotten thoughts she's been thinking about Nicky.

"He wanted to. Until you get your new fish."

"How did he ever get to sleep without Dizzy?"

"With great difficulty. He loves you, Mary Ellen."

"I love him too." Fizzy the fish! Mary Ellen had to smile. "Even if he is a worse pest than a fruit fly." She lay back on the pillow. "Mom?"

"What, honey?" Dr. Bobowick was gathering

dirty laundry from the floor and stuffing it into the pillowcase from the other bed.

"When you broke the mirror, did you have bad luck?"

"I don't remember. If I did, I probably didn't make the connection. I was never the superstitious type. My mother was, though." Now she was at the book shelf, rearranging the books into orderly rows.

"Gram?"

"Mmm-hmm. If she ever spilled salt, she always threw a pinch over her left shoulder. Supposedly spilling salt caused bad luck, but the pinch was the antidote." Dr. Bobowick swept a pile of change off the top of the book shelf. "Where's your piggy bank?"

Mary Ellen shrugged. "Under something, I guess."

Her mother looked around, spotted an empty clamshell, and deposited the change in it. Then she chuckled. "Gram used to say a little rhyme: 'Find a penny, pick it up, and all the day, you'll have good luck.' When I was mad at her for something, I used to go around the house, scattering pennies."

"How come?"

"Well, she couldn't vacuum them up, and I knew she was superstitious enough to bend over and pick up every one. Pretty mean thing to do, hunh?"

Mary Ellen smiled. "Well, maybe she did get some extra luck. Maybe if you believe in it, it works."

"There, that's a little better." Dr. Bobowick shoved the last book in properly, came over to the bed, and kissed Mary Ellen's forehead. "Okay, back to sleep. Sweet dreams till sunbeams find you."

But when Mary Ellen opened her eyes the next morning, there wasn't a sunbeam in sight. The whole world was drizzly and gray. By afternoon her throat felt better and her fever was gone. But a solid head cold had settled in. Justine called after school.

"Where were you today?"

"Sick," Mary Ellen said. "I have a horrible cold. I think the medicine I'm taking is giving me weird dreams too. Last night I dreamed that one of the fruit flies mutated into a striped octopus. It was in my fish tank, and it escaped and kept trying to grab my ankle and trip me. Only it wasn't spitting ink, it was spitting bubbles. Are the bugs any better at school?"

"Worse," Justine said. "I think Ms. P. S. is fed up with Miss Trink complaining about it. When she came in moaning about her miniature citrus today, Ms. P. S. said, 'Well, they are fruit flies. Maybe they're being fruitful and multiplying!'" She giggled.

"Did you harvest any more of the space-seeds?"

"Four more plants," Justine reported. "Ben was so funny today. He caught three fruit flies in one of those plastic gum-machine eggs and pretended he was training them. Jason called it 'Hairy Melon's Fruit Fly Circus.' You know, like a flea—"

"I know. Very funny. I'm in hysterics."

"He asked about you. Why you weren't in school."

"Jason?"

"No, Ben. Maybe he likes you."

"Right. And maybe my dead fish will come back to life and tap-dance back into the fish tank."

"Your fish died? What happened?" Justine sounded shocked.

Mary Ellen told her.

Justine was silent a moment. "Listen, are you

sure you're meditating enough on your crystal? Olivia says you have to merge your own mental powers with the crystal power through concentration and visualization."

"I'm trying!"

Mary Ellen *had* tried. She'd pictured all the positive things she could think of. Right after the bubble-bath disaster, she'd pictured her parents deciding that two kids were one too many and putting Nicky up for adoption. She'd pictured Mr. Kelly getting fired from his job so the Kellys wouldn't have to move to Paris. She'd thought long and hard about Jason coming down with a case of lockjaw so he could never open his big mouth again. And this morning she'd held the crystal in her hand for five minutes, concentrating on Amy Colter growing a wart on her nose so huge that all the powder in the world wouldn't cover it up.

"Did Amy look any different in school today?" she asked hopefully.

"Uh-uh. Unless you count the fake tattoo she had on her arm. My father would *kill* me if I wore one of those to school. If I wore one, period. Why?"

"Never mind." Mary Ellen sighed and touched the pendant. Power crystals. Of course they didn't work. But it was still a pretty necklace.

8 · BUG JUICE, SNIFFLES & SKUNKS

Mary Ellen looked with dismay at the red cuff of Ben's white sweatshirt sleeve. She was a server for Justine's bon voyage party, ladling fruit punch from the big stainless-steel bowl on Ms. P. S.'s desk. When Ben held out his paper cup, he'd smiled at her, and she'd been so taken by surprise that she'd over-ladled, spilling punch all over his hand.

"Sorry," she mumbled.

"Here are some napkins," Justine said quickly. She was standing next to Mary Ellen, cutting the bon voyage cake and handing out pieces as all the kids filed by. Ms. P. S. had brought the cake in, a big rectangle with chocolate icing and a yellow Eiffel Tower squiggled on it.

"You're such a loser, Mary Ellen," said Amy, right behind Ben and Jason in the refreshment line.

"Amy, that's not nice, or necessary," Ms. P. S. said. She grabbed a wad of napkins and sopped up the puddle on her desk.

"Hey, is that strawberry punch, Bobowick? It matches your face." Jason elbowed Ben and snickered.

"That's enough, Jason. You have your cake and punch, so take your seat. But Mary Ellen, please try to be careful. Now, I have a tape of French folk songs—let's have a little entertainment."

The whole day had been a combination geography-culture lesson about France. They'd watched a travel video about Paris, talked about French art, French history, the French Revolution. When Ms. P. S. left the room to go get the cake and the punch bowl from the cafeteria, Jason had jumped up and done a guillotine demonstration on Amy.

"Cut it out, you jerk," she'd shrieked, but she was laughing.

"She loves it," Mary Ellen had muttered to Justine.

"She'd like it better if it was Ben," Justine had whispered back. "Look at this."

Justine shoved over the big card the whole class had signed, and pointed to Amy's message, a short poem:

> In Paris, you'll meet lots of men,
> So I hope you don't mind if I take Ben!!!
> Don't forget to write and invite me for vacation,
>   Luv, Amy

"Take Ben!" Justine whispered indignantly. "Like he's a—a—"

"Hamburger and french fries to go," Mary Ellen said, nodding. "Look at that—all her *i*'s are dotted with little hearts. She's a total flirt. A floozy, Gram would call her. What I can't figure out is why all the boys like her."

Justine had shrugged helplessly.

Ben was back at his desk now, talking to Jason, who was standing in the aisle. Even though Ben was on the quiet side, compared to Jason, he was already in with the cool kids.

It was weird, the cliques had only really started last year. Before that, they had all been just fourth-graders. Now Justine was sort of a floater; she seemed to be able to hang around with any group and fit in okay. Mary Ellen, on the other hand, felt herself getting more and more stuck in the category that included klutzes, brains, and nerds. Losers. It wasn't fair. Someone shouldn't have to be stuck in a social category if they didn't want to be there. She wondered if you could escape.

"Anytime you're ready, Mary Ellen," Amy said, sounding bored.

"Sometime this year would be nice," Debra added.

Mary Ellen gritted her teeth as she filled Debra's cup first, wishing she could dump punch on both their heads. As Amy approached with her superior sneer, an irresistible impulse seized Mary Ellen. A few fruit flies had been hovering by the punch bowl. Mary Ellen had shooed them aside whenever they got too close, but one unlucky insect had gotten stuck in a drop of punch behind the bowl, where no one but Mary Ellen could see it.

She pretended to drop the ladle behind the bowl. While Amy rolled her eyes and waited impatiently, Mary Ellen flicked the fruit fly into the ladle with her fingertip. Then she carefully scooped up some punch and poured it into Amy's cup, watching as the dark speck disappeared in the red juice.

"Cheers, Amy," she said.

Three more kids to go, and Ms. P. S., and then she and Justine took their cake and punch back to their desks. As Mary Ellen passed Amy on the way to her seat, she checked the cup. It was empty.

"Hey, Amy, do you know what they call this kind of punch?"

Amy eyed her suspiciously. "What?"

"They call it *bug* juice. Think about it." Mary Ellen grinned wickedly and took her seat.

"I can't believe you really did that!" Justine was shaking her head, laughing.

"I'm glad Ms. P. S. couldn't believe it either," Mary Ellen said. "But Amy deserved it."

They sat side by side on the Kellys' lawn, watching the movers load the moving van.

"That looks like the last of it," Justine said mournfully as the men came out of the house, each carrying a few small boxes. The metal door of the truck closed with clanging finality. Just like the door of a jail cell, Mary Ellen thought. She had to serve a one-year sentence. She looked at Justine.

Justine's eyes filled with tears. Automatically, Mary Ellen's did the same.

"Don't," Mary Ellen said. "It's too hard to stop once you get started. Wait here. I'll be right back." She got up and jogged toward the house, one hand clutching her tourmaline necklace.

Inside, she snatched Justine's going-away present off the counter. She'd bought it last night at the Gardenia Gift Shop next to the Pet Gallery, when her father took her out to buy more fish. Hurrying back, she dropped it on Justine's lap. "Here."

"Hey, my favorite flavor!" Justine cheered up slightly as she pulled off the pack of sugarless watermelon bubblegum that was taped to the wrapping paper. "Plus, it reminds me of you now, you know, water-*mel*—"

"Don't say it! Anyway, it's just for decoration. But I thought it might come in handy on the airplane when your ears start to pop. Open the present."

Justine unwrapped the package and pulled out a blank book covered in flowered rose calico fabric, and a box of airmail stationery.

"Thanks, Mary Ellen. They're really nice."

"Well, I didn't want to give you anything too

big, because you're all packed. And I figured you could use the book as a diary and write down all the stuff about Paris, so you'll remember when you come back. And the stationery so you remember to write to me."

"You *know* I won't forget that."

"Look inside the box."

Justine lifted the cover and Mary Ellen tilted the top back so Justine could see the snapshot she'd taped inside, a picture of the two of them on the Bobowicks' swings, taken in fourth grade. Underneath, she'd written: BEST PEN PALS.

Justine smiled. "And best friends. No matter what."

"No matter where," Mary Ellen added.

"No matter if we have a fight."

"No matter how many miles away from each other we live."

"No matter how messy you are."

"Hey!" Mary Ellen leaned sideways and knocked Justine off balance.

"Only kidding."

"Justine!" Mrs. Kelly was calling from the front porch. "Time to go."

"You're leaving now?"

Justine waved to her mother. "I'll be right

there," she called. "We're just going to the hotel to get cleaned up for dinner," she told Mary Ellen. "We'll be back at seven o'clock."

The two girls looked at each other. Mary Ellen didn't know what to say. She swallowed.

"I asked my mother to make the lemon-ginger chicken."

Justine nodded sadly.

"I bet they won't have lemon-ginger chicken in Paris."

"So I'll send you the recipe in my first letter."

"Justine, shake a leg!" Mr. Kelly called from the station wagon.

Justine stood with her gifts in one hand and dusted off the seat of her jeans with the other. "I'll see you tonight. Thanks again, for—" She stopped, her voice sounding a little choky. "Gotta go." Then she ran for the car.

Mary Ellen watched the Kellys' car drive down the street. Slowly she got up and trudged toward the house.

In the kitchen, Dr. Bobowick was grating fresh gingerroot into a small bowl. Mary Ellen put her head down and sniffed through her still-stuffy nose. Nothing.

"I won't even be able to taste dinner." She

looked out the side window at the Kellys' house and sighed.

Her mother put down the grater and the ginger, and gave her a little hug.

"Why? Why do things have to change? I mean, it's okay if they change when they're bad. But why do they have to change when they're fine already?"

"Because that's the way life is, sweetie." Dr. Bobowick kissed the top of Mary Ellen's head. "Things change. They just do. And sometimes change can bring some nice surprises—if you try to go along with it, instead of resisting it. Now go blow your nose and wash your hands. You can help me set the table."

"So we're going to consolidate several departments, and trim the fat."

Mr. Kelly was talking to the grown-ups, while Mary Ellen and Justine started to clear the table. Mr. Kelly had been talking business through most of dinner, and from the sounds of things Mary Ellen was guessing those French workers were in for some big changes.

"Nobody ate very much," she said to Justine as they carried plates from the dining room into the kitchen. "Except Olivia. She had four helpings of noodles and vegetables."

"She's got a crystal for a healthy digestive system and a good appetite. A pinkish-orange one. The appetite part sure works," Justine said. "I wish she'd get one for energy to help with the dishes. She always sits around like she's one of the grown-ups."

"... reorganize from the top down and clear out all the deadwood ..." Mr. Kelly was still going on as the girls came back for the rest of the dishes.

"Mary Ellen, would you turn on the coffeemaker please?" Dr. Bobowick asked. "It's all set up. Just flick the switch." She looked around the table. "Anyone prefer tea?"

"Do you have any purple lotus herbal tea, Dr. Bobowick?" Olivia asked.

"I'm afraid I only have plain old ordinary tea, Olivia." Mary Ellen's mother smiled. "Would you like a cup of that?"

Olivia shook her head, looking horrified. "No, thanks. Tannic acid and caffeine."

"Oh for heaven's sake, Olivia, we're not talking about arsenic," Mr. Kelly barked. "A cup of tea is a cup of tea."

"Caffeine happens to make people very tense,

Daddy," Olivia said. "In case you hadn't noticed."

"Know-it-all teenage vegetarians make people even tenser," Mr. Kelly said. "In case *you* hadn't noticed."

"Now, now. We're all a little tense with the strain of moving." Mrs. Kelly laughed nervously, and Mary Ellen felt a little sorry for her. "Let's all try to relax and enjoy this last evening with our friends."

"I'm completely relaxed," Olivia said. She untied a small cloth pouch from the belt loop of her jeans and emptied out a dozen multicolored shiny stones. "See? This one's for inner harmony, this one's for—"

Mr. Kelly threw his hands up and rolled his eyes. "I give up!" But he said it with a smile.

"Can I see your rocks?" Nicky was off his chair and elbowing his way onto Olivia's lap, as Mary Ellen and Justine headed back for the kitchen.

"'Last evening with friends.'" Mary Ellen sighed.

"I know. But let's not think about it. We still have dessert to go."

Mary Ellen eyed the compost container as she scraped the last plate into it. "I'd better get rid of this, or there won't be any room when everyone doesn't eat their pie. Where did I put my shoes?" She scanned the room for them and spotted her mother's loafers by the back door. They'd do; she and her mother were only a size apart. Grabbing the plastic container of leftover glop, she slipped her feet in the loafers and opened the back door.

As she walked toward the garage, Mary Ellen thought that the whole day had felt like the day before a dentist appointment. You just kept dreading it. But once the dentist appointment was over, you could forget about it. When this day was over, the Kellys would be gone.

Mary Ellen sniffed and let out a long sigh. As she tipped the plastic container, sloshing the leftovers onto the compost heap, a dark shadow on the edge of the mound leapt in surprise. Mary Ellen froze. By the dim glow of the garage light, she saw a small animal doing a little dance, backward and forward, stamping its paws. There was an unmistakable white stripe down its black furry back.

Panic rushed through her. Sidestepping, she tried to escape, but her right shoe stuck in the decaying muck and her foot pulled out of it. As she hopped on her left foot, struggling to regain her balance, Mary Ellen saw the skunk's tail go up, bushy and stiff, except for the tip. Frantically she looked for a non-gloppy spot to set her shoeless foot on. A second later she was staring down at a round lifeless fish eye in a tiny black-and-white carcass next to her sock.

"AAAGH! Tiger!" Down she went on the rotting garbage with a squashy thud. The skunk's tail flipped straight up, a jet of oily fluid shot out, and a fine spray filled the air. For the first time all week, Mary Ellen could smell something—a reeking mix of garlic, burnt cork, dirty diapers, and singed hair.

Her screams brought both families running. Everyone stopped at the edge of the driveway— except Dr. Bobowick, who approached warily, squinting into the darkness.

"Come on, honey, up you go. It's gone."

Mary Ellen could tell her mother was talking just through her mouth, trying to block out the stench as she gingerly extended a hand.

"Are you all right?

Mary Ellen shook her head and struggled to her feet. As Dr. Bobowick led her away from the compost heap, everyone else backed up.

Mrs. Kelly was pinching her nose closed.

Nicky was jumping up and down in excitement. "Pee-yew! Melon stinks!"

"Don't worry, Mary Ellen," Olivia called from the hedge, about twenty feet away. "Skunk musk is all-natural."

Justine just stood there, shaking her head and saying, "This is very, very bad luck."

Dr. Bobowick spoke calmly. "Okay, why don't you all go back inside. Corinne, maybe you can serve the dessert and—"

"I think we'll just get going, Laura," Mr. Kelly said hastily. "Big day tomorrow."

"Yes, we've got to get an early start. Girls, get in the car. Thank you so much for the lovely dinner, Laura."

"Well, have a good flight," Dr. Bobowick said. "And a good year. Stay in touch."

"We will," Mrs. Kelly said.

Justine looked at Mary Ellen. "'Bye. I'll write as soon as we get there."

Mary Ellen gave her a weak wave and watched her trot down the driveway after her parents.

"Now what?" Mr. Bobowick asked, as soon as they'd left.

"Peter, can you run to the store and get tomato juice? Big cans. A lot of them." Dr. Bobowick stood with her hands on her hips, looking tired.

"Three cases of jumbo tomato-juice cans, coming right up." He jingled his keys.

"And could you—"

"Take Nicky with me, I know. Let's go, Nicko. We're on an errand of mercy."

When they were alone, Mary Ellen's mother looked at her kindly, but she didn't put an arm around her. "Do you feel nauseous?"

Mary Ellen shook her head. Miserable, but not nauseous. "I can't really smell it that much. But my hands and arms feel sort of tingly."

"Mercaptans," her mother said. "Similar chemical composition to alcohol, except the oxygen is replaced by sulfur. That's the part that—" Dr. Bobowick paused.

"Stinks." Mary Ellen finished for her.

"Stinks." Her mother nodded. "No other word for it. You didn't smell it at all?"

"Uh-uh. Not until it sprayed. I saw it, but then my shoe—your shoe—got stuck, and I lost my balance. So what do I do now?"

Dr. Bobowick bit her lip. "I don't want to bring these clothes inside. We'll bag them out here, and put them right in the trash."

"But it's my favorite shirt," Mary Ellen wailed.

"And my favorite shoes," Dr. Bobowick said, shaking her head. "But there's nothing we can do about it now. I'll run in and get a blanket. You wait on the patio, honey."

Dr. Bobowick returned a minute later with an old blanket and a trash bag. She held the blanket up as a screen while Mary Ellen got undressed.

"As soon as Daddy gets back, you'll have to take a bath and wash your hair in the tomato juice. It should neutralize most of the odor. It didn't get in your eyes, did it?"

Mary Ellen shook her head, wriggling out of her jeans.

"It's actually a lucky thing you fell," Dr. Bobowick said, as Mary Ellen stuffed the clothes in the trash bag. "The spray can cause temporary blindness. And a skunk's instincts tell it to aim for eyes."

Lucky. Ha! Lucky her favorite shirt was ruined. Lucky she smelled worse than a garbage truck. The only luck I have, Mary Ellen thought bitterly, as she wrapped the blanket around herself, is stinking, rotten luck.

9 · WHALE TAIL

"Hey, Aldrich, think fast. Heads up, Hairy Melon."

Mary Ellen ducked as something round whizzed past her.

"You guys, cut it out," Debra whined. "Give me back my apple, Jason, or I'll tell Ms. P. S. you stole it from my backpack."

"Oooh. I'm scared now." Jason grinned and held up his hands. Ben threw the apple back.

Jason zigzagged up the aisle and made a jump shot toward the wastebasket. The apple disappeared behind the gray metal can.

"No good!" Kevin Middendorf shouted, just as the bell rang.

Ms. P. S. came hurrying through the door. Casually, Mary Ellen pulled a strand of hair across her cheek and sniffed. Her nose still wasn't working at one hundred percent smelling power.

"I don't smell it anymore, honey," her mother had said that morning. "But maybe I've just gotten used to it. You can stay home from school if you want to." But Mary Ellen hadn't wanted to stay home—with Nicky at nursery school and her mother teaching—all by herself, next door to the house where Justine wasn't.

Last night she'd taken two baths in the tomato juice, long soaks—hair and all—with steamy soapy showers in between. The baths were gruesome, like something out of an old horror movie. She couldn't stop thinking about the nightmare with the giant mutated fruit fly, imagining it surfacing through the rust-colored murk.

"All right, seats everyone. Jason, that means you," Ms. P. S. said.

As Jason made his way back up the aisle, he stopped next to Mary Ellen and wrinkled his nose. He leaned down and sniffed.

"Whew! That's some perfume, Bobowick. What's it called—Eau de Sewer?"

Mary Ellen glared at him. All the kids started snickering.

"Jason ... sit ... down ... please."

Amy was leaning back in her seat, grimacing. "They have this wonderful modern invention, Mary Ellen. It's called a shower. Ever hear of it?"

"What'd you do?" Jason was going on. "Mug a skunk?"

"That ... is ... enough." Frowning, Ms. P. S. walked down the aisle, reached up to Jason's shoulders, and steered him toward his seat. Then she turned to Mary Ellen, sniffed, and bit her lip. "Mary Ellen? I don't mean to pry, but ..."

"Yes, I mugged a skunk!" Mary Ellen cut her teacher short. "Out on our compost heap. I clobbered him. Can everyone just leave me alone now?" She scowled.

Ms. P. S. nodded kindly and went back up the aisle.

"It smells like he clobbered you," Amy turned and whispered.

When Mary Ellen looked across the aisle at Justine's empty desk, it really hit her. Justine was gone. She had to fend off this ugly mob of sixth-graders all alone. Clutching her necklace, she swallowed hard.

Lunch was even more miserable than the morning. Mary Ellen couldn't taste the macaroni-and-cheese, and it felt like paste in her mouth. Justine was probably on her way to the airport right now. As she sat alone in a corner of the cafeteria, watching the big round clock, it seemed to Mary Ellen that each minute took forever to tick by. Was this day ever going to be over?

When everyone was back in the classroom after lunch, Ms. P. S. stood by the chalkboard and clapped her hands for quiet. On the floor next to her were two big rolls of white paper and stacks of newspapers. Her desk was covered with rolls of masking tape, several large plastic jars of tempera paint—black, white, blue, gray, and green—and six heavy-duty staplers.

"Clear your desks, please," Ms. P. S. was saying.

"Hey," Ben said.

Mary Ellen looked up. Was Ben talking to her? Apparently so—he was looking right at her. His expression seemed sympathetic.

"What's all that stuff for?" he asked.

Mary Ellen shrugged stiffly. She didn't want anyone feeling sorry for her right now—it might make her cry.

"As you know, every year the sixth grade goes on an overnight field trip—"

"The whale watch. Moby Dick, here we come!" Jason called out.

"That's right, Jason, the whale watch." A fruit fly wandered by Ms. P. S.'s face, and she snatched absentmindedly at the air. "In preparation for this trip, we're going to be studying whales. Today we'll do our first whale project—whales to scale."

"Whales don't have scales. They're mammals, not fish," Mary Ellen objected.

"I said, 'whales *to* scale,' not 'whales *with* scales,' Mary Ellen. Scale as in size," Ms. P. S. said.

"Oh." Mary Ellen slumped in her seat, embarrassed. She resolved not to open her mouth for the rest of the day.

"We're going to transfer whale outlines from this book to graph paper, and enlarge them according to various scales. First, let's move all the desks against the walls, so we have room to work."

Immediately, all the kids jumped up and began noisily rearranging desks. Jason bumper-carred his right into Mary Ellen's. She kicked him in the shin, and to her satisfaction saw him wince a little before he covered up with a smirk.

"We shouldn't call you Hairy Melon anymore. We should call you Smelly Ellen," he said, pushing past her.

When the desks were out of the way, Ms. P. S. read lists of names of who would work together. "Marcia Palumbo, Debra Hirsch, Jason Hodges, Ben Aldrich, and Mary Ellen Bobowick—your group will be doing the minke whale."

Mary Ellen groaned. How could Ms. P. S. be so dense—putting her in with that group? Why not just stand her up in front of a firing squad?

Debra was raising her hand. "Ms. P. S., do I have to be in a group with Mary Ellen? I have bad allergies, and skunk stink—"

"I'm sure you'll survive, Debra," Ms. P. S. said, a hint of warning in her voice.

"Then could you lend us some clothespins for our noses?" Jason asked innocently.

Ms. P. S. fixed her severest frown on him.

Mary Ellen didn't even care anymore. By one-thirty, all the groups had drawn pencil-line grids on big sheets of the white paper, traced the whale outlines onto graph paper, and transferred the outlines, enlarging them, block by block. The room filled with the sound of scissors as the groups cut out their whales, then of newspaper rustling as they stuffed them like giant pillows and stapled the edges together.

"Hey, Smelly Ellen, pass the stapler," Jason said, after checking to make sure Ms. P. S. was on the other side of the room.

"Get your own stapler and staple your teeth together, Brace-Face," Mary Ellen shot back.

"As soon as your group's whale is stuffed, take it down to the gym," Ms. P. S. said. "We'll paint them down there and let them dry over the weekend. On Monday Mr. George is going to hang them from the ceiling with fishing line. They'll stay up until after the environmental assembly in four weeks."

"We're done," Jason called across the room. "Can we go?"

"Yes, you can go. Take it downstairs—carefully! Lay it in the corner by the mats, then come back for newspaper and paint supplies."

With Jason hollering, "Thar she blows," everybody grabbed a section of whale and spread out in a line.

"I'm not standing next to her!" Debra said.

"Let Smelly Ellen take the tail. That way she'll

be behind us and we won't have to walk through the—"

"That … is … e-nough … and … I … mean … it." Ms. P. S. folded her arms. The room went silent.

"How do you think you're making Mary Ellen feel? I want to see some maturity in this classroom, starting *now.*"

All the kids stared at their shoes. This was as mad as Ms. P. S. ever got. While Mary Ellen appreciated Ms. P. S. sticking up for her, she had a sinking feeling that it wasn't going to improve her popularity rating.

"I'll take the tail, I don't care," she mumbled, and went to the end of her group's line.

They marched clumsily through the halls, Mary Ellen keeping her head down. As they approached the double fire-doors that led into the gym, Mary Ellen felt a fierce spasm of missing Justine, and had to blink back tears. She reached for her necklace—as Ben followed Jason through the door, holding it open with his foot, until Marcia could catch it with hers. Debra was struggling right in front of Mary Ellen with her section of the bulky paper mammal. Gone! The pendant wasn't hanging around her neck! Mary Ellen let go of the tail and frantically patted the front of her shirt to see if it had dropped inside.

"Look out!" Debra squealed.

"My crystal. It's gone! Did anybody—"

Her question was cut off by the thud of the heavy door closing, along with a ripping sound. "—see it?" she finished weakly.

She looked down. There was the tail of the unpainted whale, on the floor. She looked up. There were the kids, standing on the other side of the fire-doors, glaring accusingly through the glass. A little phrase started echoing in her head: Smelly Ellen, the Whale-De-Tailer.

Mary Ellen sat at the kitchen table, her chin in her hand, gazing bleakly at the Kellys' empty house. Dr. Bobowick sat across the table from her, paging through a scientific journal. It seemed so impossible that Justine was gone. All day long Mary Ellen had had little starts, when a thought flitted through her mind, and her automatic reaction was to turn and whisper to Justine. Her absence was almost more solid than her presence would have been.

The other kids seemed to have forgotten about her already, regrouped and closed their circle, with

Mary Ellen definitely on the outside. On the way home from school, it was Amy and Ben, and Debra and Jason, unbelievably enough. Mary Ellen had walked behind them, but she'd been close enough to pick up snatches of their conversation. They were making plans to go to the movies that night.

"My mother's driving, so we can pick you up, Ben," Amy had said.

"Whoa, a date," Jason teased.

"Shut up, Jason," Amy said, but Mary Ellen could tell she wasn't mad. "So we'll pick you up at seven o'clock, okay, Ben?"

Amy's tone of voice was sweeter than corn syrup. It made Mary Ellen want to gag.

Now she doodled on a blank page in her history notebook: tiny minke whales, some with tails, some without. It was so unfair. How unlucky could one person get? Mary Ellen wondered if there'd ever been a survey done on how many people actually experienced bad luck after breaking a mirror. What were the statistics? Could you measure luck some way? Seven years. Multiplied by fifty-two, that made 364 weeks. Multiplied by seven, that made 2,548 days. Multiplied by twenty-four hours in a day, that made—a lot. She was too depressed to work out the rest of the math. No matter how you looked at it, it was a lot of bad luck.

"I'm doomed." She let out a long sigh.

Dr. Bobowick looked up, startled. "Excuse me?"

"I said I'm doomed. Mom, do you believe in curses?"

Dr. Bobowick closed the magazine.

"Curses?"

"I mean like superstitions. Like if you step on a crack, you'll break your mother's back. Or if you walk under a ladder, something bad will happen. Or—"

"If you break a mirror, you'll have seven years' bad luck?" Dr. Bobowick finished for her, then smiled. "No, I can't say that I do, honey, speaking as a scientist."

"But all the bad things started happening right after I broke the mirror. And the fortune cookie predicted it."

"What fortune cookie?" Her mother looked confused.

"The night of the Kellys' party. When Justine slept over and we had Chinese food. My fortune said to reflect carefully, or my deeds would bring bad luck. Then I broke the mirror. The Kellys going away, the fruit flies, getting sick and not smelling the skunk, and today, the necklace and the whale tail. You can't tell me that's not the worst string of bad luck you've ever heard of."

Dr. Bobowick put her palms down flat on the table. "Okay, let's analyze this. The fortune cookie? Freak coincidence. Weird, but not statistically impossible. The mirror? Cause and effect. Glass plus slippery hands equals broken glass. Now, the fruit flies? You tripped and dropped the jar. The skunk? You slipped and fell. The whale? Clumsiness, again. How many inches have you grown in the past six months?"

Mary Ellen thought. "About three and a half, I think."

Her mother nodded. "And your shoe size jumped too. I've had to buy you three new pairs of sneakers in the past year. So you've just been through a real growth spurt."

"That's why I'm such a klutz?"

"I'm sure it has something to do with it. If I recall, sixth grade was the year that everyone in my family was convinced I was accident-prone. That's the year I rode my bike into a telephone pole and needed stitches, sprained my wrist falling down the stairs, and dislocated my shoulder while ice-skating."

Mary Ellen was silent for a moment. It made some sense, she guessed. "How long did it last?"

"A few months. You just need some time to grow into yourself. In the meantime, try to be a little extra careful."

"Okay. But what about the bubbles and my fish? And the Kellys moving? And my necklace?"

Dr. Bobowick tilted her head and smiled. "The Kellys moving has nothing to do with you, honey, in the sense of bad luck. Mr. Kelly had mentioned the possibility to your father and me over the summer. I never said anything, because it wasn't a sure thing. But that was all set in motion before you broke the mirror. So, what else?"

"The fish," Mary Ellen prompted.

"The fish?" Her mother smiled. "Nicky's interpretation of your explanation about aquariums, I'm afraid. Unfortunate, but if you think about it, logical, to a four-year-old."

"Well, losing the necklace was definitely bad luck."

"I suppose so, honey, but a lot of people lose jewelry. It's not a unique occurrence."

Mary Ellen sighed. "It wasn't working, anyway. But still, it wasn't just any old necklace. I wish I hadn't lost it."

Dr. Bobowick reached across the table and patted Mary Ellen's hand sympathetically. "It was sort of a talisman, wasn't it?"

"What's a talisman?"

"A power object. People believed in them before they knew anything about science and about why things happen. Back then life seemed full of uncontrollable forces. Talismans were a primitive attempt to control those forces."

"If it's such a primitive belief, how come they sell power crystals today?" Mary Ellen asked.

Her mother looked thoughtful. "I guess a lot of aspects of modern life seem beyond human control too. But I still think if there's any 'power' in these modern talismans, it lies in giving a person a positive attitude. Which is another thing. You've heard about the power of positive thinking. I think there's probably a power of negative thinking too."

"Expect bad things to happen and they will?"

"Self-fulfilling prophecies." Dr. Bobowick nodded. "Subconsciously, you can boost things in the wrong direction. Now does that dispel your fears about being jinxed?"

"I guess, kind of." Mary Ellen chewed on the end of her pen.

"Good. Then can you set the table for me? There's a department meeting at the university tonight, so we need to eat early."

"Okay." Mary Ellen got up from the table and moved her books over to the counter. "So you don't think I'll have any more bad luck, then?"

Dr. Bobowick had risen, and was rummaging in the freezer, pulling out a package of chicken. "I certainly hope not." She popped it in the microwave and set the defrost timer, then rapped her knuckles three times on the butcher-block cutting board. "But knock on wood."

Mary Ellen grinned. "What was that for?"

Her mother looked down at her hand in surprise. "Oh. Well!" She laughed. "I suppose it doesn't hurt to be on the safe side."

10 · Best Pen Pals

Hôtel Meurice
Paris, France
September 24th

Dear Mary Ellen,

Well, here we are in Paris! We're staying at this hotel until our apartment is ready. It's pretty cool—we have two huge rooms with really high ceilings and lots of gold-painted molding and a marble bathtub—pretty *ooh-la-la!* And there's a little refrigerator with fancy snacks and champagne and stuff. Dad went straight for the pâté, but then Olivia told him how they make it, by pumping fattening food down the throats of these poor geese. She said he was about to eat the diseased liver of an animal that had been tortured, then sacrificed, for middle-class gluttons. He got so mad he almost threw the jar off the balcony, but my mother stopped him. She said he might be arrested for littering, or for beaning some French pedestrian with a pâté jar, and what if French police didn't understand how mad radical vegetarian teenagers can make a person?

Me, I'm sticking to omelettes, pizza, Coca-Cola, and salads, the only things I recognize on menus so far. (I think of you whenever I see a tomato! How's the fruit fly situation?)

I start school next week. It's not a French school, though, it's a special one where a lot of American and English kids go. So even though I'll be learning French, my regular classes will be in English. (I wonder if there'll be any cute guys. Speaking of which, how's Ben?)

From what I've seen, the French people don't seem very friendly. I really hate feeling so stupid when I can't figure out what they're saying. I'm not sure I'm going to like it here. Write back SOON!

Love, your best pen pal,
Justine

P. S. Is the crystal working?

Same old house I've
always lived in, USA
September 29th

Dear Justine,

I really really REALLY miss you! A new family's going to move into your house on Monday, so I won't be able to pretend you're just on vacation anymore. My mother told me they're from Cincinnati and they have four boys! (But no eligible ones—a fourth-grader, a first-grader, and three-year-old twins.) I hate them already. (Well, not really, but I know I'm going to want to go over and say, "Get out of Justine's house!")

None of my new fish have died yet. I haven't named them, because once you name them, you start to get emotionally involved. I'm not ready to risk it until they've survived for a couple of weeks.

School is horrible times ten. No, times infinity. I'll give you three reasons: 1) Jason 2) Amy 3) No you.

But at least the fruit flies are starting to thin out some. Five more sets of NASA seeds harvested, only five plants to go. Miss Trink brought in some Venus flytraps today, those bug-eating plants. That should be interesting! But at least she's stopped spraying garlic all over the place.

Sorry this letter isn't very long, but there's not much going on around here. WRITE BACK ASAP (as soon as possible).

Love, your best pen pal,
Mary Ellen

P. S. In case you were wondering, tomato juice gets MOST of the smell of skunk-stink off.

• • •

193, rue St Jacques
Paris, France
October 4th

Dear Mary Ellen,

This is my new address, so you can send my letters here, now, instead of my father's office. Our building is really old. There's a big wooden door painted black that you open and drive your car right through, and park in this courtyard. Our apartment is on the third floor. All the floors are slanty. You practically have to walk uphill to go look out the window!

Did you know the French sell all their different kinds of food in different stores? We drove by a store called a *poissonnerie*. Can you imagine having a store just to sell poison?! Like I said, the French don't seem very friendly. We went to a *boucherie* yesterday, which is a meat market. (Hey, boucherie—like butcher, I just realized.) Anyway, they had all these skinned rabbits in the window. My mother said maybe we'll try it—after all, when in Rome, do as the Romans do. I said, "We're not in Rome, we're in Paris. YOU do it! No french-fried bunnies for me!"

There's lots of outdoor cafés in my neighborhood, where student types hang out. Olivia found one that serves herbal tea and stuff like wheat-germ-bran-honey-yogurt muffins. That's where she goes after school. Guess what—and you have to promise not to tell, or I'll have to give the money back. I was walking home from the *boulangerie*. (That's the bakery—you say it "boo," like a ghost, and "lingerie," like a fancy nightgown.) Anyway, I saw Olivia sitting at a table under an umbrella with this really cute guy and she was SMOKING A CIGARETTE. She didn't see me, but I told her later that if she was being a vegetarian for her health, smoking was pretty stupid. She said she knew, but when he offered her one, she didn't know what to say. I told her, just say *Non*. (That's French for no.) Anyway, she gave me twenty-five francs (about five dollars), not to tell, and I already spent it, so …

School's okay, but it's school. Although there is a kid whose father works at the Embassy who's pretty *beau*. (That's French for cute—for a guy. Did you know everything is either masculine or feminine in French? Cabbage is masculine. Bicycle is feminine. Every single noun and there's no clue so you have to memorize them all!) Anyway, the *beau* guy's name is Robert, and he's been here for three years and talks like a native. I think I might need some tutoring! WRITE BACK.

Amour,
Justine

• • •

October 9th

Dear Justine,

The new neighbors are HORRIBLE! Especially the twins. They're bigger than Nicky, even though they're younger. The first day they moved in, they pushed Nicky down in the compost heap. The second day they tried to run him over in the driveway with their Big Wheel tricycles. The third day they kidnapped Dizzy and painted his head with peanut butter. Gram said she's going to have to teach Nicky some more advanced karate moves. Mom said she didn't know if that was such a great idea.

Guess who I walked home from school with yesterday? Ben! (I hope you don't mind. How's Robert?) Anyway, it was only by accident. Jason's mother picked him up for an orthodontist appointment, and Amy was out sick, yesterday and today. (Ha-ha-ha—I hope it's a fatal case of pimples.) And we just happened to be going in the same direction—did you know he lives three blocks away from us? Well, from me—for this year, anyway. He and his mother and father are living with his grandparents because his father lost his job in California, and they couldn't afford their house anymore. Talk about some serious bad luck. He seemed really different without Jason and Amy around. Like he might even be nice.

Miss Trink's going crazy because even though there are no more space-tomato plants, and she brought her miniature citrus trees home to fumigate them, we still have fruit flies in both classrooms. Today she brought in one of those canister vacuum cleaners with the long hoses, and she was VACUUMING the bugs! You should have seen it when she got the hem of her dress caught. Ms. P. S. had to help her pull it out of the hose. The whole class cracked up as soon as she went back to her own room, even Ms. P. S. But she said vacuuming is actually one technique environmentalists use, part of a thing called IPM—Integrated Pest Management, which is keeping pests under control without using pesticides. I wonder if there's an IPM technique for rodents like Jason Hodges!

Let's see, what else. We're all getting ready for the huge environmental assembly the whole school's putting on at the end of next week. Every class has to do a skit or reports and wear environmental costumes. I think I'm going to be a tree and talk about the greenhouse effect.

I guess that's all for now. WRITE QUICK! TPJITSWY. (This place just isn't the same without you.)

Love,
Mary Ellen

· · ·

October 14th

Dear Mary Ellen,

They're environmental over here too! We were out taking *une promenade* (a walk) last Sunday, and these two guys were dressed in special wet suits at the Place de la Concorde. They pumped the suits full of air, then climbed in the fountain. Olivia talked to some of their friends and found out they were protesting to clean up the Seine so that river seals, one of their endangered species, would come back. They looked more like giant penguins than seals to me, but it was funny to see them paddling around in the fountain. My father says that's all he needs, for Olivia to get hooked up with a bunch of kooky French teenagers.

After that, we took a cab to the Eiffel Tower and I threw up on it. Well, not on the whole thing, just in the elevator. I was okay going up to the first level, and we had a snack in the cafe and the view was really cool. Then we went all the way to the top. When I went near the edge, it felt like the whole thing was tipping over. So I moved back to the middle, but I was starting to feel awful, so we got in the elevator to go down, but it was too late. The Coca-Cola and *saucisse* (hot dog) stayed up while the elevator went down. But you know the funny thing? I thought all French people were cranky and couldn't stand Americans, but one lady gave Mom her plastic shopping bag for my coat, and a man said, *Pauvre petite,* which means "poor little girl," and put his newspaper over the mess on the floor. (He was being so nice, I didn't take offense about him calling me "little girl.") And when we got to the bottom, a security guard asked if I needed a doctor, and then he got a cab for us.

Remember that kid Robert I told you about? Okay, now forget him. He's a Jason. He gave me a croissant that he'd filled with really hot French mustard. But there's a kid who lives in the apartment building next to ours. His name is Guy. (It rhymes with "key," not "buy.") He smiled at me three times—it's nice that you don't have to be a genius to translate smiles. And yesterday we talked. His English is a lot better than my French. I was asking him about the poison store, and he told me they don't sell poison at a *poissonnerie,* they sell fish!

(Dead ones.) (For eating.) Anyway, I'll keep you posted on developments.

Beaucoup de l'amour,
(Lots of love)
Justine

P. S. How was Friday the 13th? Did the crystal help?

· · ·

October 18th

Dear Justine,

I guess my luck might be getting a little better. I didn't want to tell you this before, but I can now, because I found it—my tourmaline. It fell off while we were making these big stuffed paper whales to hang in the gym. I felt SO bad. I looked all over, but I couldn't find it. Anyway, Mr. George took all the whales down from where they were hanging from the ceiling, because one of them fell down on a volleyball team and the gym teacher said they were nice decorations, but they constituted a hazard. Poor Ms. P. S. was so depressed. Anyway, we took the whales apart and unstuffed them so we could just tape them on the walls like murals, and guess what? My necklace was stuffed inside the minke! The clasp was broken. (I'll get it fixed.)

My tree costume for the assembly is finished. (Apple tree.) I painted this huge piece of cardboard from a refrigerator box, and cut out branches, and glued paper leaves on. And I cut out a hole in the foliage part to stick my face through. It's so tall that I have to stand on a chair behind it. Jason said Ben should be a fruit fly and buzz around my branches. Ben got all red. Amy looked really mad, and she said I should get some fertilizer, if I wanted to grow some real apples, or else I should be a raisin tree. And THEN, Ben said raisins don't grow on trees, and she got even madder!

We're having a feud with the new neighbors. The TT's (Terrible Twins) were ganging up on Nicky with these machine-gun water pistols. So he bopped one with Dizzy and karate-chopped the other and chased them both home, yelling *KEE-AI.* Their mother came over to tell my mother how irresponsible it was to teach a four-year-old karate, and my mother said it wasn't as irresponsible as letting a pair of three-year-olds run around the neighborhood like terrorists with toy machine guns.

Then she (the lady) called Nicky a little bully, and my mother called them (the twins) little thugs. I have a feeling it's going to be a long year.

WWW. (Write, write, write.)

Love,
Mary Ellen

11 · Fruit Flies Again

"I couldn't believe it! His mother is a cashier at SaveMart. That is *so* tacky."

From the next row of lockers in the girls' locker room, where everyone was changing into their costumes for the assembly dress rehearsal, Mary Ellen could hear Amy and Debra giggling. She'd worn her green turtleneck and brown corduroy pants to school, so she didn't actually have to change clothes. Sitting on the narrow bench, she squinted into the mirror of her mother's compact, and dabbed pink and red on her cheeks.

"How did you know it was her? How did she know it was you?" Debra asked.

"When my mother used her credit card, I guess she recognized the name. She thanked my mother for driving us both ways to the movies, and said it was hard, with her working most evenings."

The movies. They must be talking about Ben's mother.

"What about his father? Couldn't he drive?" Debra was asking.

"I don't know. Ben told me he mostly sits around watching TV and being depressed about losing his job and his house."

Mary Ellen stopped dabbing and listened harder.

"Did you see what he was wearing today?" Debra was still giggling. "SaveMart-brand blue jeans."

"I know. Maybe his mother gets a discount off the discount because she works there," Amy said. "I'm going to dump him, anyway. He didn't even pay for my ticket at the movies. Jason paid for yours."

Mary Ellen's jaw dropped. Amy had always been mean, but this was worse than mean, it was—vicious. Even though the comments hadn't been aimed at her, they made her feel terrible. Her ears almost felt dirty from what she'd overheard.

Amy and Debra walked past on their way out

of the locker room. Amy was dressed as a starfish. Specks of red glitter dropped off whenever she moved. Debra was wearing blue tights and a blue leotard, with flaps of filmy fabric sewn on. She was the ocean.

"That's a good way to cover up your freckles, Mary Ellen," Amy said. She and Debra laughed.

Mary Ellen sat stone-faced, not answering, until Amy shrugged.

"Come on, Debra. I want to practice my poem one more time."

After they left Mary Ellen slowly finished putting her face paint on, adding a few patches of green so she'd look like a McIntosh. From her bag she pulled a tube of flavored appleberry lip gloss that she'd found at the drugstore, and put it on. She'd thought she was getting used to Justine being gone, but sometimes it really hit her. Was it as hard to be the one to move to a new place as it was to be the one left behind? With a sigh, she went back to the classroom.

"Take your places, please," Ms. P. S. was saying.

Mary Ellen dragged her tree trunk up from the back of the room and pulled Ms. P. S.'s chair out from the desk. The hole for her face was up in the foliage. Her place onstage was in the back, but hers was the tallest costume. Ms. P. S. had told them the mayor was definitely going to be there, along with a reporter and photographer. If there were pictures in the newspaper, her tree costume would definitely be visible. That would be fun to send to Justine.

In front of Mary Ellen, Amy and Debra took their places, Debra waving her filmy flaps like waves. Ben was to their left, in a gray cardboard nuclear reactor with a crack down one side. Mary Ellen thought about Justine again and wondered if Ben had a best friend back in California. Jason, next to Ben, was in a cardboard barrel painted to look like pesticide, with a huge skull and crossbones on the front. Marcia was on Mary Ellen's other side, dressed as a tree, too, but a smaller one, some kind of palm. Her costume was covered with long strands of tinselly stuff, to look like a tropical rain forest. Mary Ellen wished she'd thought of that. An apple tree was so ordinary.

From the back of the classroom, Ms. P. S. was directing kids to move a little this way or that.

"Starfish, could you move a little closer to Nuclear Power Plant, please?"

Amy shifted toward Ben, jostling his reactor.

"Sorry," Ben apologized. "This thing is kind of

bulky." He smiled at Amy, who turned away. Amy leaned toward Debra and whispered, but not so softly that Mary Ellen couldn't hear.

"At least it covers up the SaveMart blue jeans."

Mary Ellen couldn't see the front of Ben's face, but she saw red creep up the back of his neck and his ears, so she knew he'd heard too.

"Hey, Amy," she said softly. "You shouldn't have been a starfish. You should have been a shark. Except that would be an insult to sharks. And if you think SaveMart's so tacky, what were you doing shopping there, anyway?"

Amy and Debra both turned around and glared at Mary Ellen.

"For your information, Mary Ellen, her mother only buys socks and underwear there," Debra said. "Right, Amy?"

Now Amy glared at Debra. "Would you shut up, you idiot?" Debra looked hurt.

"Underwear?" Mary Ellen said, raising her eyebrows. "Well, some people think what's underneath is as important as what shows." She stared straight ahead, but out of the corner of her eye, she caught Ben shooting her a grateful smile.

"Everyone … quiet … now … please." Ms. P. S. waited for all the chatter to stop. "All right.

Starfish and Ocean. Begin, please."

Amy took a deep breath and launched into her poem:

There's a big problem
In the ocean.
Oil spills pollute it
Like gooey lotion.

Mary Ellen rolled her eyes. Gooey lotion! If she had to listen to Amy's stupid poem one more time, her brain was going to be polluted. She stretched her neck a little. It was starting to get stiff from stooping to keep her face in the opening. She should have made the hole about four inches higher. As Jason went into his hazardous waste speech, a fruit fly looped around in front of Mary Ellen's face, hovering near her mouth. Puckering her lips, she blew it away. It was incredible. All the space-tomato plants has been gone for over a week, but there were still a few fruit flies hanging around. What were they living on, air?

As Ben went into his part about the potential dangers of nuclear power, the fruit fly returned.

"Shoo!" Mary Ellen whispered, and blew it away again. The scent of her appleberry lip gloss must be attracting it.

"Mary Ellen, it's your turn!" Marcia was poking her in the ribs.

"Oh. Okay. Um." Mary Ellen could still see the fruit fly wandering around the fake foliage near her face.

"Mary Ellen?" Ms. P. S. said. "All parts were supposed to be memorized by today."

"I know. It is. I mean—" Taking a deep breath, Mary Ellen started her report. "If it weren't for trees, there would be no life as we know it on earth. We owe the air we breathe to trees." She stared at the back wall, trying to ignore the persistent little speck that was going after her lip gloss. Now she couldn't see it, but it was down there somewhere, between her chin and her nose. "The cycle by which carbon dioxide is converted back to oxygen is an essential process—" It tickled against her nose, and she snorted violently, out, then in. "Aaagh!"

Her nose! The fruit fly was in her nose! Mary Ellen's hands flew up to her face.

"Stupid bug, I'm not a real apple tree!" The chair was tottering as Mary Ellen's branches tilted into Marcia's rain forest.

"Look out, Mary Ellen! You're ripping my rain!"

Ripping her rain? Who cared! A fruit fly was inside her face and she had to get it out. Snorting and sputtering, Mary Ellen stepped backward. There was a flying tangle of arms, legs, and cardboard, as she fell off the chair. The apple tree fell forward onto the ocean and the starfish.

"Tim-ber!" Mary Ellen heard Jason shout, as a pain unlike anything she'd ever felt shot through her right leg, just above the ankle.

"Get your stupid tree off me, you idiot." Amy's voice, muffled, came from under the cardboard.

"My rain is ruined," Marcia whined.

"Get off me! Get off!" Someone was sitting on Mary Ellen's leg.

"Is everyone all right?" Ms. P. S. was on her knees, trying to sort out the pile of kids, props, and costume wreckage. Reaching out a hand, she helped Debra up, off Mary Ellen's leg.

Miss Trink had appeared by the door.

"Really, Ms. Purcelli-Smith, if you cannot control—" Then she spotted Mary Ellen. "Oh dear," she said.

Tears were rolling down Mary Ellen's cheeks, mixing with the makeup so her whole face felt gummy.

Ms. P. S.'s exasperated expression turned to one of concern.

"Can you get up, Mary Ellen? Here, let me help—"

"No, I can't, don't move it. It hurts." Mary Ellen was sobbing now. She didn't even care if the whole class saw her crying.

"I'll go get the nurse," Ben volunteered, running out of the room.

Mary Ellen's leg felt like it was on fire. She lay there while all the kids stood in a half circle around her, staring. She sniffed, and her nose still tickled. A fruit fly. In her nose. *Eeee-ew!*

"Ms. P. S.?" she choked out.

"What, Mary Ellen?" her teacher asked anxiously.

"Could you please get me a tissue?"

"Mary Ellen." Someone's voice was calling her out of a sleep so deep it seemed bottomless. Mary Ellen tried to open her eyes. Uh-uh. Too bright. Her mind dove back down. "Mary Ellen," the voice persisted, following her into the warm, painless grayness. "Mary Ellen, wake up, honey."

This time she squinted. Where was she? She closed her eyes again. A hand was holding hers, and another hand was smoothing back her hair. She was in a bed, but it wasn't her own. The hospital.

Now she was beginning to remember. Gram had come to school, because the school couldn't get in touch with either of her parents. She remembered one of the paramedics carefully cutting off her sock and the leg of her brown pants with a pair of shears. Her ankle was swollen and already turning purplish-blue. They'd strapped a rubber splint to it before carrying her to the ambulance on a stretcher.

Once in the emergency room, it seemed like she had to wait forever. Finally a nurse took her down to the X-ray department on a bed with wheels. They covered her up with a heavy apron filled with lead, except for her legs and face, then went and hid behind a wall while the X-ray machine made Star Trek noises.

Back in the emergency room, the doctor came in and said that Mary Ellen's leg was broken right above the ankle. A fractured fibula, he called it, and explained that they had to put Mary Ellen under general anesthesia to set the bone.

They waited some more, while the hospital tried to reach Mary Ellen's parents for permission to treat her. Gram argued with the doctor and nurses about not keeping a child in pain waiting for some dumb formality. "I'm her mother's mother, and her mother will do what I tell her to do."

Gram got so loud that a nurse told her she'd have to leave if she wouldn't stop disturbing the patients. Finally the hospital got through to Mr. Bobowick, and he faxed his signature over for permission to fix her leg, and said he was on his way.

"Mary Ellen, we're here, sweetheart. Can you open your eyes?" Her father's voice.

"Mmm-hmm," Mary Ellen murmured. She tried to shift in the bed. Something heavy was holding her leg down. The piercing pain seemed to be gone, replaced by an ache. What else had happened? Mary Ellen tried to focus her thoughts.

The operating room. Big faces with paper masks, all eyes and foreheads, stood over her. One of them put something over her mouth and nose.

"It's only oxygen," one of the nurses said. "You're going to feel a little pinch in your arm." The nurse was holding her arm still, swabbing something cold on it. Ouch! That was more than a pinch. Hands restrained her from sitting up.

"Count backward from ten." The nurse was nice, but very bossy. Mary Ellen tried to obey.

"Ten, nine—" And that was all. Until now.

Groggy, but awake, Mary Ellen opened her eyes.

"Hi, Daddy," she croaked. Her mouth and throat were dry. "I broke my leg."

"So I'm told." He squeezed her hand. "How's it feel?"

"Better than before. What time is it?"

He checked his watch. "About five-thirty."

She'd fallen off the chair just before lunch, so that meant she'd been here for about five hours. It seemed like a lot longer.

"Where's Mom? Did they find her?"

"She's down in the cafeteria, cooling your grandmother off. Gram was a little hot under the collar by the time we showed up. They'll be back in a few minutes." He winked at Mary Ellen.

"What about Nicky? Did you bring him?"

Her father shook his head. "He's next door with Mrs. Alexander and the boys."

Mary Ellen raised her eyebrows. Nicky with the thugs and their mother?

She only had one more question. "When can I go home?"

"Soon," Mr. Bobowick said. "Definitely tonight. The doctor wants to see you again, and the nurse said they have to keep you until all the effects of the anesthesia have worn off."

Mary Ellen's eyelids slid closed, then opened again as Dr. Bobowick and Gram slipped through the white curtain, holding cups of hot coffee.

"Mary Ellen, you're awake! I'm sorry, I just ran down to—" Her mother stepped up to the bed and leaned over, hugging her carefully. "My poor baby! How do you feel?"

"Okay, but I'm really thirsty."

Her mother nodded. "They're getting you some ginger ale. After you drink a whole can—if it agrees with your stomach—and after you go to the bathroom, they'll let us take you home."

Ginger ale, that sounded good. Mary Ellen's lips were chapped. She tried to lick them, but her tongue was dry too.

Her mother noticed. "The anesthesia dehydrates you some."

"I'll go hunt down that ornery nurse and tell her to move her buns, my granddaughter's parched." Gram left, frowning and shaking her head.

"And I'll go check and make sure all the paperwork is taken care of, so we can spring you as soon as they give the word." Her father patted her shoulder and followed Gram out.

"Is your head clearing up?" Dr. Bobowick asked.

"I think so." Mary Ellen still felt a little floaty, but other than that, not too bad. As long as she didn't try to move her leg, it didn't hurt.

"I'm sorry I wasn't home or at my office when this happened, honey. I was in the library, and then I went straight downtown to do some errands. I picked Nicky up at nursery school, and it was three-thirty by the time I got home. The phone was ringing off the hook when I came in the door. Your grandmother."

Dr. Bobowick rummaged in her big pocketbook, and brought out a flat package, gift-wrapped. "A get-well present," she said, handing it to Mary Ellen.

"What is it?"

"Open it and see." Dr. Bobowick smiled.

Tearing the wrapping paper off, Mary Ellen opened the box and removed a thick wad of tissue paper. There was her great-great-grandmother's mirror. She took it out of the box, and turned it over. The glass was new.

"Ugh," she said, looking at her reflection. The face paint was only partly cleaned off, so she had red and green streaks over her freckles. Stripes over dots! She had to grin.

"I guess I didn't get it repaired quite in time to prevent this latest disaster. But now you should be okay," her mother was saying. "I'm sure replacing the mirror cancels out any residual bad luck. All right? No more bad luck? Please?"

Mary Ellen set the mirror down on the blanket and shook her head. "It wasn't bad luck."

Her mother looked surprised. "No? What was it?"

"Simple cause and effect. Cause—a fruit fly flying up my nose. Effect—me falling off the chair trying to get it out. Remind me never to do an apple-face makeover again, okay?"

12 · A Change of Fortune

"Special Delivery for Mary Ellen Bobowick!" Mr. Bobowick came into Mary Ellen's room, holding an enormous basket of fruit with a big red bow tied to the handle.

"Who's that from?" Mary Ellen looked up from the drawer of her night table, which her mother had taken out and put on the bed so Mary Ellen could clean it. Four-fifths of the contents were now in the trash bag next to her bed.

"Mr. Ellsworth just dropped it off," her father said. "When Gram and Nicky were down there this morning, Gram noticed some fruit flies and mentioned your accident. I guess Mr. Ellsworth felt guilty for giving them to you in the first place."

Dr. Bobowick turned away from Mary Ellen's desk, which she'd just finished straightening.

"What I don't understand is how there could have been any fruit flies in that classroom when the tomato plants had been gone for two weeks."

"Maybe there was something in the space-tomatoes that made them live longer," Mary Ellen suggested. "Hey, maybe they're a new strain of super fruit fly!"

Dr. Bobowick looked worried for a second. "I think it's unlikely. Highly unlikely." She shook her head. "Still, if there are any left when you go back to school, maybe you could bring me a specimen." She pointed to the basket Mary Ellen's father was holding. "In any case, Peter, please, bring that basket downstairs and leave it on the back porch. I'm going to scrub every last grape."

Before he left, Mr. Bobowick took a look around the room. He let out a long whistle. "What happened in here?"

"We cleaned it," Mary Ellen told him. "Well, Mom did most of the work."

"Not bad. And it'll stay that way for a week, anyway, with you bedridden."

"Dad!"

"Only kidding." Her father winked and left with the basket. Mary Ellen handed the nearly-empty drawer to her mother, who fitted it back in its slot.

Together, with Mary Ellen directing from the bed, where both her head and her leg were propped up with pillows, she and her mother had overhauled the whole room. Everything either found a place, went on a give-away pile, or into one of three huge trash bags.

"Do you need to save these?" Dr. Bobowick held up four wooden chopsticks that had some-how found their way under Mary Ellen's radiator.

"Oh, keep those, they remind me of Justine and the night we had Chinese—" Mary Ellen stopped. The night of the fortune cookie. Did she want a souvenir of that? "You can toss them, Mom. They give you new ones every time, anyway."

While Dr. Bobowick vacuumed, Mary Ellen took her aquarium notebook from the night table, where her mother had neatly stacked some books, new stationery that Gram had given her, a deck of cards for solitaire, and a pack of markers so people could sign her cast, all placed within easy reach.

• • •

Saturday, October 21
  A. Observations
    a. Some new algae growth on rocks.
    b. Fish One and Fish Two are definitely tougher than Fish Three and Fish Four.
    c. Their stripes make them look like little prison inmates.
  B. Questions
    a. Should I name them Jailbird and Mugsy?

Mary Ellen started to nibble at her thumbnail, then snatched it away from her mouth as soon as she realized what she was doing.

"There! That's that." Dr. Bobowick unplugged the vacuum and rolled up the cord.

"Thanks, Mom," Mary Ellen said gratefully, surveying her room. "I wouldn't have known where to start."

"It was definitely a two-person job. I was afraid if you had visitors, they might call the Health Department. Very bad for my reputation."

Mary Ellen smiled.

"Would you like a snack? Mrs. Alexander sent over some brownies."

"Mrs. Alexander? Are you friends now?"

"Well, she's not Corinne, and I don't know her very well yet. But she was so nice the day you got hurt. She was in the Kellys'—I mean her—backyard, and she heard me telling Nicky we had to go to the hospital. She came right over and offered to help."

"Brownies would be good," Mary Ellen said. "With milk?"

"Coming right up." Her mother lugged the vacuum away.

Mary Ellen surveyed the orderly room. It made her brain feel sort of peaceful. Maybe there was something to be said for organization.

A few minutes later, Nicky came in. "Here's your brownies, Melon." He crossed the room slowly, with careful little steps, carrying a half-filled mug of milk in one hand, and a small plate with two brownies in the other. "I brought it upstairs all by myself."

"Good job, Nicky."

"Mrs. Alexander made them. She let me and Timmy and Tommy help." Mary Ellen grinned. So, TT could stand for Terrible Twins or Timmy and Tommy.

"Do you like them? The twins?"

Nicky screwed up his face, thinking. "They're okay. They're better when we're playing than when we're fighting." He wandered over to watch the fish.

Mary Ellen took a bite of brownie and a sip of milk, then set the snack on her night table. Twisting, she took her new stationery, a pen, and a book to lean on, and started a letter to Justine.

Dear Justine,
    You'll never guess what happened on Thursday.

She wrote out the whole story, including Amy's snotty comments about Ben.

    So okay. I'm not cool. But if it means being that horrible, I think I'll skip it.
    You should see the pajamas my mother bought me, in case anyone comes to visit. They're kind of purple, with tiny ivy leaves and ruffles around the neck. And a bunch of pairs of HUGE socks, to wear over the cast so my toes don't get cold. I have a purple one on now. The doctor said I have to rest for a few days, then I'll be on crutches for two weeks.

After that, he's going to put a little rubber thing on the bottom of the cast, so I can walk around on it.

This was going to be a long letter. There was the fixed mirror, the neighbors turning out okay, Gram switching from karate class to water ballet at the Y.

"Up for a visitor, honey?" Dr. Bobowick popped her head through the doorway.

"A visitor? Who?"

Mary Ellen's mother smiled mysteriously and left. Quickly Mary Ellen picked up the mirror from the night table. She checked her teeth to make sure there weren't any brownie crumbs stuck, and noticed that her freckles were fading some, the way they always did when summer was over.

"This way, Ben," she heard her mother say from down the hall.

Ben? Mary Ellen felt her cheeks get warm. Why was Ben here? He appeared in the doorway, looking just as uncomfortable as Mary Ellen felt. Dr. Bobowick was next to him, and Nicky was peering around her legs.

"Who are you?" Nicky asked. "Are you Melon's boyfriend?"

"Nicky! Mom, would you—"

Ben smiled down at Nicky. "I'm in your sister's class."

Dr. Bobowick hustled Nicky away, and Ben stood uncertainly in the doorway for a minute.

"Um, want to sit down?" Mary Ellen pointed at the desk chair.

Ben crossed the room, avoiding her eyes, and put a pile of schoolbooks with some papers sticking out of them on Mary Ellen's desk. Then he sat, looking at his shoes.

"Uh, Ms. P. S. asked if someone would bring your work home, so I said I would, because I walk right by your house ..." His voice trailed off.

"Thanks," Mary Ellen said.

"There's a card. We all signed it."

"Um, thanks," Mary Ellen said again. "That's nice."

"It's the second card. Ms. P. S. didn't like what Amy wrote on the first one, so we did a new one."

"What did she write?" Mary Ellen could imagine, but she was curious. "One of her stupid poems?"

"Yeah. I don't remember exactly."

Mary Ellen thought he might be lying about that, so he wouldn't hurt her feelings.

"Thanks for what you said," he went on. "I mean, about—" He stopped, and Mary Ellen saw him glance at his blue jeans.

"That's okay," she said quickly.

Now Ben looked down at his shoes again. "Listen, there's something I want to tell you. Remember Career Day, when you fell and your jar broke?"

Mary Ellen winced. She'd just as soon forget it. Now Ben was looking at her.

"I remember."

He took a deep breath. "It was really *my* fault."

Mary Ellen looked at him blankly. "What do you mean?"

"Well, I thought your report was cool and the flies and all—and you looked like you felt really bad, so I was trying to get your attention, to say, you know, 'good going,' or something. Anyway, I stuck out my foot and that's why you tripped and the jar broke. But I wasn't trying to trip you. Really." He finished what he was saying in a rush and looked at Mary Ellen apologetically.

Mary Ellen blinked, astonished.

"So I wanted to say I'm sorry about what happened, and that it wound up making you break your leg."

"That's okay." Mary Ellen smiled. "I'm glad you told me, though. I was starting to think I was the world's biggest klutz, or else totally jinxed."

Ben smiled back, then laughed a little. "Oh, and we finally found out where the fruit flies were coming from."

"Where?"

"An apple. That day we were fooling around with Debra's lunch—"

"And Jason missed the basket. That apple was still around?"

Ben nodded. "It rolled under the bookshelf near the window. It was starting to smell—that's how Ms. P. S. tracked it down. Boy, talk about some larvae!" He looked around Mary Ellen's room.

It was lucky she and her mother had just excavated it, Mary Ellen thought. Lucky—there was that word again. She almost giggled.

"Hey, is that a saltwater fish tank?"

"Yeah." Mary Ellen nodded, surprised again. Most people didn't know the difference between a freshwater and a saltwater tank.

Ben got up and went over to look. "Damsels, hunh? You going to put any bigger fish in there?"

"Next month. I haven't decided what kind yet, though." Mary Ellen watched him watch her fish.

"Angelfish are pretty hardy. Or yellow tangs. They'd be good. Once you start forking out a lot of money for tropical fish, you want to make sure they're not going to die on you, if you can help it."

"'If you can help it' is right," Mary Ellen said. Ben looked confused, so she told him about Nicky and the bubbles. He laughed, but he seemed to understand what a traumatic experience it was.

"About new fish—what I meant was you have to get fish that get along together, that aren't natural competitors for food or territory," he explained. "I have a book I could lend you if you want." His voice was full of more enthusiasm than Mary Ellen had heard in the whole time he'd been at school.

"That would be great. How do you know so much about it?" Mary Ellen asked curiously.

"I used to have my own tank. We sold it when we moved. As soon as my father gets a job and we move into our own house, I'm gonna get a new one."

Now Mary Ellen picked up a touch of sadness in his voice. "You can visit mine, if you want."

"Thanks. Hey, I was thinking, if you're going to be out of school for a few days, I can drop your work off, you know, on my way home." He sounded nervous again.

"That would be great," Mary Ellen said. She had to bite her cheeks to keep from grinning. Ben dropping by to visit every day! Wait till she wrote *that* to Justine!

Ben was looking around the room now, as if he didn't know what to say next.

"Well, I guess I'd better get going." He started for the door, then stopped and pointed at Mary Ellen's cast. "Want me to sign it?"

"Uh, sure. Okay." Mary Ellen handed him a purple marker. He took it and scrawled his name right above the sock. Then he looked straight into her eyes and smiled.

Something inside Mary Ellen fluttered in a funny way. A good way. She smiled back.

Ben straightened up and grinned. "See ya." Then he was gone.

Mary Ellen heard him bound down the stairs and say good-bye to her mother.

She leaned back against her pillows. Her face

wouldn't stop smiling. After a minute, she snatched up the letter to Justine.

You are never, ever, EVER going to believe this!!!

She scribbled furiously.

And he says he'll bring my schoolwork over every day until I get back. Hey, do you think this is what they call a change of fortune?

Read All the Stories by
Beverly Cleary